BY MUR LAFFERTY

MOJANG
MINECRAFT™
THE LOST JOURNALS

MOJANG

MINECRAFT™
THE LOST JOURNALS

MUR LAFFERTY

DEL
REY

NEW YORK

2021 Del Rey Trade Paperback Edition

Copyright © 2019 by Mojang AB and Mojang Synergies AB.
MINECRAFT and the Minecraft logo are trademarks of
the Microsoft group of companies.
All rights reserved.

Published in the United States by Del Rey,
an imprint of Random House, a division of
Penguin Random House LLC, New York.

DEL REY is a registered trademark and the CIRCLE colophon
is a trademark of Penguin Random House LLC.

Originally published in hardcover in the United States by Del Rey,
an imprint of Random House, a division of
Penguin Random House LLC, in 2019.

LIBRARY OF CONGRESS CATALOGING-IN-PUBLICATION DATA
Names: Lafferty, Mur, author.
Title: Minecraft: the lost journals / Mur Lafferty.
Description: New York: Del Rey, [2019] | Series: Minecraft
Identifiers: LCCN 2019007452| ISBN 9780399180712 (trade paperback) |
ISBN 9780399180705 (eBook)
Subjects: | BISAC: JUVENILE FICTION / Action & Adventure / Survival
Stories. | JUVENILE FICTION / Media Tie-In. | JUVENILE FICTION /
Fantasy & Magic.
Classification: LCC PZ7.1.L224 Los 2019 | DDC [Fic]—dc23
LC record available at https://lccn.loc.gov/2019007452

Printed in the United States of America on acid-free paper.

randomhousebooks.com

4 6 8 9 7 5 3

Book design by Elizabeth A. D. Eno

For Fiona, Blaze, Alex, and all the turtles

@MOJANG

MINECRAFT™
THE LOST JOURNALS

From the lost journal of N▮▮▮

Today I nurse the considerable burns I received when encountering ▮▮. And I barely made it out alive. It was a yellow monstrosity, a cube surrounded by ▮▮▮▮

I foolishly thought that my shirt would be good enough, thinking this was just a scouting mission. The promise of strong ▮▮▮ and other riches are too tempting to ignore.

But wool armor is not a thing that exists, despite what ▮▮▮ insisted. My shirt protected me from nothing. I'll have to tell ▮ that they were wasting their time.

And I'm sorry for the lost wool.

And the lost sheep.

I did find something of interest: ▮▮▮▮▮ but it was guarded by those fire things. I will have to get more data before I face them again.

Now to sneak to the village to see if someone will trade a healing potion with me. I hope I don't run across ▮▮▮▮▮

I couldn't face them right now.

I think I have perfected building the portal. Almost nothing went wrong this time. I did have the problem of zombies on this side, and on the other side there were more of those terrible fire creatures. But hey, when life gives you mushrooms, you make mushroom soup. I made a small platform and brought a great deal of cobblestone through to build a safe area.

I think I am making progress.

Why write things down if you don't intend anyone to read them? And yet I hope no one reads this. I've been attacked by more creatures on the other side, and barely escaped with my life. If I can't find a safe place to live there, I will certainly die. But living on this side is no longer an option.

If you do find this journal, don't follow my lead. The danger is high and the risks are many. The only treasure I've gotten is a block of material that burns me when I touch it. Nothing valuable is on the other side.

Right now, I seek only freedom.

PART ONE

CHAPTER 1

MIGHT AS WELL RAISE MOOSHROOMS

Orange and red heads bobbed up and down in the local cove, bleating as they surfaced and gurgling when they sank. Alison shook her head. The sheep had gotten loose and gone straight for the water. Again.

She crossed her arms and watched their fuzzy square heads appearing and disappearing in the water, showing no sign that they were considering coming to dry land anytime soon. What was with these sheep? They wanted to be in the water more than any sheep she'd ever known. Her parents had bred the animals for their coloring, but as far as she knew, they hadn't tried to cross-breed with squid.

Speaking of squid: from the dark smudges in the water, the sheep had attracted some friends.

The sun hung high in the sky, so Alison had time to wade in and get them, but she hated swimming after the little monsters. Wet wool was the worst smell.

"Fantastic," she muttered, pushing her sleeves up. She pulled some wheat from her pack and walked to the edge of the cove.

"What's up?" came a voice over her shoulder.

She jumped and whirled. Her best friend stood behind her, head cocked. "Max!" she shouted. "Don't do that. I thought you were a creeper!"

He shrugged. "Was I hissing? I just wanted to know what you were up to." He leaned to look around her. "Oh . . . sheep swimming again?"

She was torn between pointing out the stupidly obvious and telling him to get away from the water. She decided on both. "Apple and Lil' Prince got out again. I'm getting them back"— Max opened his mouth, but she continued, hurriedly—"alone, Max. Your mom will kill you if you go near the water again. And then she'll kill me twice."

He looked around with exaggerated focus, shielding his eyes from the sun with his hand. "Hm. I don't see her anywhere. And I'm already near the water." He edged closer and dipped his toes in, eyes squeezed shut. Then he opened them. "Did I die?"

"Not yet," Alison said through gritted teeth. "Just let me get them out of there. If you want to help, go check their pen or something. Figure out why they got out again."

Max took another step into the water, watching the animals splash around. Alison had to admit, the sheep did look like they were having the time of their lives in the cove. A squid had definitely joined them, its tentacles waving in and out of the water alongside the sheep's brightly colored heads.

"You know they like me better than you," he said. "You need my help."

"That makes no difference, they'll come if I've got food," Alison said, exasperated. "And no, they don't like you better."

But they did. It really annoyed her that the red and orange line of her family's flock liked her best friend and ignored her. Today was no different; they must've thought Max was coming to play with them, because the moment he was up to his knees in the water they bleated happily and began to swim toward him.

He hadn't even tried to get their attention with wheat.

"Max!" came a loud shout, and Alison winced. She didn't turn around. She knew that sound very well; Max's mom made it all the time. "Get out of the water right now!"

She brushed by Alison without a word and ran into the water. Apple and Lil' Prince bleated in panic and turned to escape, eager to get away from the rampaging, splashing monster that bore down on Max. The squid dove into the deep.

Max's mom paid no attention. Max had barely begun to protest when his mom grabbed him around the middle and muscled him back toward the beach.

Max struggled. "Mom, it's okay, I'm not drowning, I wasn't going any deeper!" he shouted. "Alison needed help with the sheep!"

"I will not risk losing you again!" his mom said, tears already forming in her furious eyes. She dumped him on the sand and put her hands on her hips.

"You won't lose me!" Max said, but his last words were cut off with a grunt when his mom bent over suddenly and grabbed him again, wrapping him in a tight hug.

"Did you forget I almost lost you already?" she repeated, ignoring his struggles.

Alison looked away, embarrassed. In recent months, seeing others' family closeness, even the weird closeness Max had with his overprotective family, made her uncomfortable.

"And Alison," Max's mom said, letting her son go and putting her hands on her hips again. "I thought you knew better."

"Don't yell at Ali, Mom," Max said, stepping between them. "She told me not to go. I didn't listen."

"She should still take care of you. She's older."

"By less than a year!" Max protested. "I'm twelve, I don't need her to be my babysitter."

"We will talk about this at dinner, you two," she said, then pointed at Max. "Don't go into the water again."

Max sighed. "Yeah, okay. I'll go check the pens, Ali, and be really careful not to go near any water on the way. I don't know what I'll do about my spit, though. It's pretty hard to avoid." He spat on the ground and then sprinted away from it, arms flailing in mock panic.

"That's not funny!" Max's mother called as she watched him go, tears dribbling down her face. "I don't want him near the water," she reminded Alison—as if she'd forgotten.

"I know," Alison said. "I don't want to be near the water either. But the pen broke again, and I had to get the sheep back."

Max's mom wiped her cheeks and took a deep breath. Composed, she looked at Alison, pity in her swollen eyes. "Why?" she asked gently.

"Why what? Why do I need them back? Because they got out," Alison said, blinking at her. "Why did the pen break? I don't know. But I do know the sheep get out, and when that happens, you put them back in. My grandfather had a stupid saying about it, something like 'When the sheep get out, might as well raise mooshrooms.'"

Max's mom frowned. "That makes no sense. I meant why worry about the sheep? They'd do fine if you let them go wild. You don't need to care for them anymore. We don't need the wool, you don't need the responsibility. There's definitely no reason to keep breeding them, and fixing the pen just takes you back to your house over and over again. You could do without the memories, you know." She put a little emphasis on *over and over*, reminding Alison that going back to her destroyed house wasn't doing her any good. She patted Alison on the shoulder. "Think about it. I'll see you at dinner."

Alison stared into the water to avoid watching her go. The pen had been a ways from the house, through a copse of trees, so when she visited the sheep she didn't actually see the ruined tree house that she used to call home.

She visited the pen often, trying to be responsible for the sheep. She felt she owed them that much.

But Max's mom was right. They didn't need the wool anymore. And Alison was wasting time and materials with frequent repairs on the pens, and losing whole afternoons running after the lost flock.

Then again, they were one of the few sources of joy in her life. She gazed out at the swimming sheep, who happily played with the squid, which had resurfaced and was playfully wrapping its tentacles around Apple. Lil' Prince was trying to head-butt the tentacles that got near him.

Alison heard thumping steps behind her and, before she could turn around, Max was back, running past her toward the cove. With a whoop he jumped into the shallow water, making the biggest splash he possibly could have, and waded with high, galumphing steps toward the sheep, who greeted him with happy bleats.

Alison laughed and waded out after him, waving the wheat over her head. Even with the threat of getting in trouble hanging over them, Max could always make her laugh and forget about her problems for a moment.

CHAPTER 2

ALISON'S DAD WASN'T IMAGINATIVE

Apple nibbled on the wheat Max offered as Alison surveyed his fix to the sheep pen.

"Don't feed them too much," she warned, not looking around at him. "They shouldn't breed right now. I definitely don't need any more lambs."

"Aw, come on, you want a baby Apple, right?" Max said, patting the sheep. "Maybe make an Orange?"

"Not if Orange is going to be even more interested in escaping for an afternoon swim," she said. "So . . . did you use my tools to fix the pen, or did you go . . . another way?"

Max glanced up. She was frowning at the large, bulky objects he'd chosen to patch the sheep pen with. "Oh, that. I just took some blocks and plugged the hole. I couldn't find any wood. I made the fix two high just in case Big Blue started jumping again. That was right, wasn't it?"

"But . . ." she waved her hand at the fence, at a loss for words. She looked around the clearing. Alison's family's farm was outside the village, near Max's house, and their clearing was large, surrounded by tall trees. Her family's ruined tree house lay around the bend, and Max noticed she always kept her back to that area, lest she remind herself it was there.

"You had plenty of wood! I gave you good tools!" she said, waving her arms at the trees. "But you just plugged the hole with . . . what *is* that?"

"It's obsidian." Max knew she had never seen obsidian in real life. It was too rare, and their parents would never let them play around lava.

She stared at him blankly and then started firing questions at him. "How is *this* a reasonable fix? It's not even a fence anymore. And where in the Overworld did you get *obsidian*? And why would you waste *obsidian* on a sheep pen? If your mom finds out you've been messing with water and lava, she's going—"

"—to kill me, I know," he interrupted, grinning at her. "Mom will have to kill me lots of times if she finds out what I've been up to. Do you think she'll be madder about the water, or the lava?"

There. He'd left her an opening. *Ask about the blocks. Ask about where I've been.* He waited for her to ask him more, but she just herded some of the sheep back into the pen while the other sheep (Big Blue, Old Blue, Light Blue, and It's Okay You're Gray, I Still Love You, or "Okay" for short) watched them warily. Most sheep avoided the water, and avoided those who didn't avoid the water. Apple and Lil' Prince didn't care, though, munching on grain and dripping water on the grass. The air started to smell of wet wool.

Alison took her shovel from her pack and began digging in front of the fence. Max groaned. She was determined again.

"If you're bored, why don't you help me?" she said, tossing him her shovel and retrieving another one. "Dad always said moats were ugly. But I think it will be the easiest way to keep them in the pen."

Max took a moment to admire the craftsmanship of the shovel she had tossed him. When she wasn't fussing over the sheep, Alison had been throwing herself into crafting, making better and better tools every day. She had begun to dabble in armor creation, but only when they found enough materials, and there were rarely enough materials.

He got to digging, moving around the fence in the opposite direction from Alison so that they met on the other side, each having dug a one-block trench. "You going to fill it with water? Or better yet, lava!" he said, grinning.

"Not today," she said, putting her tools away. "The trench will work for now." She jumped out of it and sighed, dusting her hands off. She turned to him. "Well? Where did you find the blocks? I know you didn't mine them, because you don't have a diamond pick."

Yes! She is interested! He chuckled in what he hoped was a clever and wicked manner. "I'll tell you someday soon. And I was hoping *you* could make me a diamond pick."

She began walking back toward Max's house. "To mine obsidian you have to have a diamond pick. You need diamond to make a diamond pick, so you have to find diamond and happen to have an iron pick."

"Which should be enchanted, I know," Max said, rolling his eyes. She had told him this before. He knew they'd make a great team—she could make the tools and he could enchant them—but Alison for some reason always said that messing with enchantments was a bad idea. "But, you know, if you come across the means to make an iron pick, you *could* make one. That's all I'm saying. And that's another step toward mining our own obsidian."

She had perked up when he'd hinted about having the resources necessary to make an iron pick. After a moment, she shook her head and laughed softly. "I guess I'm predictable. Should I ask your mom to grab me some diamond when she goes to the village to see your dad next week? And then you can tell me where to find this obsidian that needs mining."

"I'll tell you later about the obsidian," he said. They were nearing his house, and if his mom overheard anything about mining, or enchanting, or doing anything else dangerous like breathing the air outside of the house, she would have another fit.

Max relaxed a little bit. He'd finally made Alison smile, a job he'd had to throw more and more effort into lately. He couldn't blame her for her grief, though. A few months ago, his own family had gone through some unfortunate changes, and it had taken a while to get used to it.

On top of that, he never expected that Alison would become essentially his adopted sister. You expected your friends to hang out, have adventures, run from zombies if you stay out too late. You don't expect them to come and live with you after a life-changing disaster like losing your home and family to an unexpected creeper attack.

Max had been grateful for her joining the family when she did, though. A few weeks before her tragedy, he had nearly drowned swimming in the cove, and ever since then his mom had been smothering with her concern for him. She'd even built a shed in the backyard to store all of their liquids away from the house, which Max thought *might* be a bit of an overreaction, though he'd never say that to her. When Alison came to live with them, stunned and grieving, it gave Mom somewhere else to channel all her worry, and Max was able to recover in peace. The best and worst part had been that Mom saw Alison as an older sister/

babysitter—worst because *come on*, Max didn't need a sitter, and best because he finally got to leave the house again, and with his best friend.

He had gotten over his near-drowning incident, but Alison understandably still had her moments of sadness over the loss of her family. Max tried his best to distract her in those times, like breaking the fence so the sheep would get out and she could have a solvable problem instead of the unanswerable storm of grief.

He'd never tell her the fence was his fault, of course. She might get mad.

When Alison had moved in, Max's mom, an architect, had welcomed her by building a tower connected to the back of their house for her to live in. It gave Alison a special place to retreat to when she needed alone time, and was cooler and more elaborate than a plain old bedroom. Max had tried to hide his jealousy at the time; his parents had never thought to put their amazing architectural skills behind making *him* a unique space that was all his own. Then he remembered what Alison had gone through and why she might need her own haven, and he got over his angst.

Sort of.

After the adventure with the escaped sheep, and after a dinner where Max and Alison assured his mom that they and the sheep were just fine, he made sure his mom was asleep, and then crept to Alison's tower door. He knocked softly.

Alison peeked out, coal smudged on her face. "What?"

"What are you crafting?" he asked eagerly, immediately forgetting the reason he was visiting.

"Shhh, come inside," she said. He gave a quick look behind him and then followed her to the staircase. Instead of up the stairs, she went to a door she had placed in the wall under the stairs and opened it. It led straight into the hillside behind Max's house; he and Alison had regularly been clearing out the area to make a secret crafting fort.

The fort had a crafting table that he had made for her soon after she'd moved in. She'd been pretty listless and unhappy, and Max had finally told her to distract his mother for fifteen minutes. Alison asked something about the skill of building in mid-air, something his mom excelled at, and as she talked, Max had snuck out to the shed to use his mom's crafting table. He'd presented the new crafting table and a few basic tools to Alison later that night, and she had smiled for the first time since moving in with them.

From then on she had something to focus on, something to do rather than wander around, grieving. They had immediately started collecting wood and stone and seeing what they could do with it. In one day they'd built their own workshop in the hidden cave they'd dug beneath the tower.

Since then, Alison had gotten quite good at crafting, repairing, and upgrading items. Tonight, Max saw that their workshop was cluttered with a number of new items. Alison had been busy since dinner! New shovels, axes, pickaxes, fishing poles, and buckets sat on the table. She picked up one shiny pickaxe and handed it to him proudly. "I found some iron," she said. "Now go find some diamond so I can make you a diamond pickaxe."

"You went mining for iron without me?" he demanded. "Why would you do that?"

His face lost its happiness and she glared at him. "To surprise you with a new pickaxe, you ungrateful dummy." She turned her back to him and started to put the tools away in the chest by the crafting table.

His outrage deflated. "Thanks," he mumbled. Eager to change the topic, he went over to the chest where they typically stored their materials. "So, uh, what else did you find?"

She didn't answer right away, so he opened the chest and stared at the contents. She had managed to find iron, sand, and coal in her excursion, but hadn't hit any of the choice blocks he'd only heard of veteran miners finding: gold, emerald, diamond, and lapis lazuli.

"You should go replace your mom's tools with the new stuff while she's asleep," Alison said, still not looking at him. They'd secretly been upgrading Max's mom's tools, and replacing the broken ones. It gave them a place to put all the extra stuff Alison was crafting just to get more experience.

He'd clearly struck a nerve, but wasn't sure what he had done. "Hey, Ali, I'm sorry. It's just fun to go mining with you, that's all. I don't like missing out."

She rubbed a hand over her face the way she remembered her mother doing and turned to him again. "I know. But . . ." She swallowed, then continued, "My dad used to get mad and say that I wasn't grateful for the things he did for me. I thought he was being mean. Now I know how he feels. Felt, I mean. And I can't apologize to him."

Shame flooded Max, making his ears burn. He looked at his grief-stricken friend, stuttered out an apology, took the offered tools, and left her alone with her tears.

Which only shamed him more. Why couldn't he just be grateful for the gift she'd given him? He was good at distraction, like letting out the sheep and giving presents. But he knew sometimes Alison needed him to just listen when she was feeling raw and unhappy, and that was the hardest thing for him to do.

CHAPTER 3

WHEN LIFE GIVES YOU LAVA, MAKE LAVA JUICE

It was weird to see both sides of the argument, Alison mused that night. She remembered the sting when her father had snapped at her, but now she understood what it was to do something nice for someone and have them toss it aside like yesterday's pork chops. She couldn't sleep, so she got out of bed and watched a skeleton wander around the clearing down below her window.

She went downstairs to the workroom and checked her supplies. She had just enough iron left to make a pickaxe for herself, so now she and Max could mine that much faster together. She pulled out a map she had been painstakingly drawing. She had placed the house and the tower against the hill, and estimated the hill's total volume.

She'd found veins of coal and iron, and marked where she had discovered each. She thought that if they went west, under Max's mom's pumpkin farm, they might find some better blocks. She hadn't shown the map to Max yet, but might tomorrow. If they made up, that is.

The pickaxe lay on the workbench, strong and well made. Alison stroked it for a moment, proud of her craftsmanship. She had never really felt that being a sheep rancher or tailor was her calling, as much as she loved the fuzzy nuisances, but this—crafting these tools—felt right.

Max's mom hadn't noticed yet that they had been secretly replacing her worn tools with Alison's upgrades. Or she hadn't said anything, anyway. And Max's mom wasn't someone who held anything back. Alison admired that, even when most of what Max's mom said had to do with overprotecting Max. There were far too many times Alison didn't say what she thought. *And even months after the accident, you'd think I wouldn't care what I said to people.*

What was she afraid of? She'd already lost nearly everything. But the answer was obvious: all she had left was Max's friendship and his family's hospitality. And she couldn't bear losing that.

The next morning, Max's mom said their favorite words. "I'm going into the village to see your dad today. Don't leave the house."

Max's family had an odd setup, with his mom in the house working on her architectural designs, and his dad staying in town for the last few months to manage a huge building project there. When Alison had asked about it, Max's mom had gotten taut around the eyes and said he had to take on extra work, then changed the subject. It felt like she was hiding something from Alison.

Max didn't like to talk about why his parents were working and living apart either, dodging the subject when Alison had asked about it, and she wondered why they'd all become so tight-lipped and somber. Max's family used to be a large, happy, boisterous group, often coming over to Alison's house for large dinners. They would sometimes bring Max's aunts and uncles, as his uncles Nicholas and Maximilian and Aunt Horty also lived in the area. The times Uncle Nicholas came over, Grandma Dia would complain and fight with him, and they'd contradict each other, but her mother always said the families were very close—not in spite of the older generation's bickering, but because of it. Alison didn't understand that at all, but she missed those times.

She obviously didn't know all the details of Max's current home life, but she wasn't going to push Max if he didn't want to talk about it. Alison knew expressing his feelings wasn't Max's strong suit, so she would wait until he was ready. Until then, they had adventures to go on.

"Are you going to be okay going by yourself?" Alison asked Max's mom.

Max's mom smiled, puzzled. "Of course. I go alone every trip when Max is in school."

Alison dropped her eyes. "I know. It's just . . . there are dangerous mobs out there."

"Ah," Max's mom said. "I see. Well, you don't need to worry about me, dear. I can handle myself just fine out there. And besides, I'll be back before nightfall." She gave Alison's arm a pat, and then went back to preparing for her trip. Alison pushed down the fear that was roiling in her stomach over the thought of Max's mom being on the road alone.

She'll be back before nightfall, Alison repeated to herself. *Everything will be fine.*

As Max's mom bustled around the kitchen collecting supplies

for her half-day journey to the village, Alison's and Max's eyes met across the table, instantly forgiving each other and making their usual plans without speaking. A few weeks back, they'd already decided that if they mined the hillside behind the house, that wasn't *technically* leaving the house. They were just excavating an area that they could turn into more rooms for Alison's tower, right?

"She will totally buy it," Max had said confidently, but Alison wasn't so sure. Still, the call of more crafting supplies was too strong to ignore.

They helped his mom pack up their donkey, Francine, with several tubes of blueprints and some food for the road, then waved her off with a promise to stay "inside." His mom stopped briefly to check the growth of her pumpkins.

Max's mom often spoke of how well her garden had grown this year, but she was disappointed that the gourds weren't quite ready to sell at the market yet. She bent down and patted one fondly, assuring it that she'd take it to town next time.

Max rolled his eyes at this. Alison knew he hated pumpkins and all dishes that had them as an ingredient, but it wasn't a vegetable Alison had eaten much of, so she still enjoyed the family's pumpkin dishes.

Max's mom straightened and frowned at the dense copse of trees that had grown between the garden and the hill behind the house. "We need to trim these back when I get home," she said. "But wait for me, don't do it yourself." And then she was off.

"Be careful!" Alison called after her.

"Finally!" Max said as his mom headed off down the path, leading Francine. "She's gone." He raced down the hall to his room and returned with a couple of torches and his new pickaxe.

"I've been working on a map," Alison said, and pulled it out of her pocket. "Here's where we've dug out so far, and I'm thinking this might be a good place to go." She moved her hand to the spot below the pumpkin patch. "I think if we go a few blocks deeper than we've already been searching, we might find better stuff."

"Let's go!" he said, heading for the door.

"Hang on—what if we find something nasty down there?" Alison asked. She always asked this, because she knew that finding a cave full of zombies and skeletons was more likely than finding a vein of gold this close to the surface.

"We run," he suggested with a grin, like he always did.

Alison mined like an ant. Max mined like a grasshopper. She did it methodically and carefully, and Max dug wherever he felt like.

Alison always worked in a grid pattern, moving forward for sixteen blocks, over for two, and then back for sixteen. Whenever she decided to go deeper, she did so carefully, creating a sloping passage and never digging straight down.

Every time she traversed these paths, she thought about making some stairs, and then at night when her legs weren't aching with the effort of jumping up on blocks, she figured it would be a waste of time and resources.

Max just dug.

When they had first started excavating, Alison immediately had to stop him from digging straight down, pointing out that he didn't know what kind of cavern he might fall into, and reminding him that if he fell, getting back up would be tough. Max then had to show off that he had perfected the art of jumping up and placing a block underneath himself to slowly build a pillar and rise within the hole he'd dug. Alison's older sister, Dextra, had used that procedure once, and then had promptly fallen off and needed medical attention. Seeing the technique again was so upsetting that she had spent the rest of the day not talking to Max.

Or so she had planned—and then she saw the sculpture of a sheep he'd made out of blocks of red wool outside her window. The statue had a silly face that surprisingly looked very much like her sheep Apple.

And now, Max didn't dig straight down anymore.

Inside the hill, Alison checked her map by the light of the torch ensconced in the wall. "We need to dig in that direction to get under the farm," she said, and Max started picking away at every block ahead of him, tunneling a large hole in the hill. She sighed and stepped a few blocks down, and then began digging her next grid.

Max snaked his tunnel in and out, messing up her grid and calling out joyfully whenever he found something that wasn't stone or dirt. Alison worked carefully, gritting her teeth and continuing her regimented excavation, marking her map. At the end of this, she would have to go through Max's haphazard mess and try to include that on her map.

She was still digging and thinking about her map when three things happened at once:

> 1: Max shouted that he'd gone too far and opened up a spot in the hill high above the pumpkin patch. Alison was vaguely aware of the daylight coming in, and turned around to see what he was doing.

> 2: Her iron pickaxe efficiently laid waste to the sandstone in front of her, and she mined without thinking

while looking over her shoulder. She opened her mouth to yell at him to plug that hole so his mom wouldn't see they'd been digging, but was overcome by heat and red light in front of her. She shielded her eyes and stumbled back, her eyes stinging from the pain.

3: An arrow twanged into the wall on her right. The cave that she'd opened was apparently full of lava and at least one skeleton armed with a bow. Two more arrows followed the first one. *Okay, definitely more than one skeleton,* she amended.

She scrambled backward, even as Max was calling her name again.

"Ali, did you hear me? I found the pumpkin patch! We're just above it!"

Lava began to leak from the cave while more arrows bounced off the wall behind her. Skeletons began walking toward her, avoiding the lava but clearly intent on punishing Alison for breaking into their home uninvited.

Alison got to her feet. She spared one final glance at the advancing mob of skeletons, then turned and barreled toward Max. He didn't have a chance to ask any questions before she grabbed him by the arm and fled through the hole he'd created.

"Maybe she won't notice," Max said, looking below them.

From their safe perch atop a tree in the stand of oaks Max's mom wanted to cut down, they looked across the pumpkin patch.

Skeletons, at least twenty, patrolled the farm in the safety of the shaded area. They avoided the center of the patch, which now was nothing but a smoking pool of lava that smelled vaguely of burnt pumpkin pie. They wandered directly under Max and Alison, the only good news being that they couldn't see the kids through the branches.

"The only way for her to not notice is if you almost drown again," Alison suggested, sitting with her knees up to her chin. "Think we can make that happen?"

Max glared at her. "I'm not the one who opened up the room to the lava and skeletons and fire and pain! And why didn't you just plug the hole? You're carrying enough blocks, aren't you?"

"See how fast *you* think when you're dodging arrows and streaming lava!" she countered. "I was just trying to get away!"

"Face it, Ali, you opened the way to that cavern and now Mom's pumpkin patch is destroyed," Max said.

"You opened the hole in the hill," she countered, but there wasn't a lot of strength in her words. She was torn between rage at Max and fear that he was right. What would happen when his mom got home? Would she ground Max and kick Alison out? How could she ruin her host's trust in her so much?

"We could get rid of the skeletons before she gets home," Max said thoughtfully. "Then we would only have the lava to deal with."

"Fight skeletons. In lava. You can't even fight a sheep!" Alison said.

Max went red. Ali didn't often bring up the time when Okay the sheep had butted him in the back and tossed him into the water trough, but when she did, it got to him. He prided himself on being really good with the sheep, but that one just didn't like him, and she made it known when she could.

"Only 'cause I didn't want you to have to explain to your dad why you'd brought home a bunch of wool and mutton that night," he mumbled.

"Besides," she said, "we don't have weapons. What are we going to do, throw dirt at the skeletons?"

Max lifted his pickaxe. "I didn't say we would fight the skeletons. I said we would get rid of them." And he started hacking away at the tree's branches.

Alison realized with pride that she had done a good job making the pickaxe: it barely looked used. It would make a good headstone for their graves after trying to fight skeletons in lava, she thought grimly.

Below them, sunlight started to peek through the holes in the foliage and fall onto the patrolling skeletons.

CHAPTER 4

YOU CAN'T SHOOT LAVA

Max hacked away at the tree's branches with the pickaxe. He would have preferred to have a regular axe, but he figured if he asked Ali to try to craft something right now, she might shove him out of the tree for his trouble.

The shaded area shrank as he chopped, and skeletons had to choose either stepping into the lava or stepping into the sunlight. Max whooped as the first skeleton got edged out of the safe shade and into the afternoon sunlight. It burst into flames and picked up speed, running around frantically looking for more shade.

Max's whoop turned to a cry of alarm as an arrow streaked past his head and got lost in the tree's branches. "Look out, Ali, they're mad!" he yelled, and kept hacking away at the tree. The sun was going down, and if they were still up here when night fell, then the skeletons would be able to wander freely around the farm.

And his mom might come home then. He'd been so preoccupied with the fear that she would catch them and punish them that he hadn't thought of the actual danger they had created.

Maybe the best thing would be punishment, because the worst would definitely involve his mom ambushed by a mob of monsters on her way home. "We gotta get rid of them before Mom gets home!" he yelled, hacking faster.

Ali wasn't behind him anymore. He figured she must be hiding in the tree, protecting herself from more arrows. He'd have to save them both, then.

His chopping efforts were rewarded by several more skeletons bursting into flame, and a few who wandered into lava, but it was too slow, he was losing his race with the sun, and he thought he heard a donkey's brays drifting down the path.

"Alison? Help!" he said as the first skeleton stepped out of the safety of the tree's shadow into dim light . . . and nothing happened to it. The sun had sunk enough, and they were safe to emerge from their shadows.

The others took their cue from the first and stepped out, finding a better angle from which to fire arrows at Max.

He turned to jump into the foliage to hide with Alison, but she was right behind him, holding something.

"Here," she said, thrusting the thing into his chest. It was a bow.

With her other hand she handed him three arrows. "Be careful, these are all we have." She held up her own handful of arrows. "I can only grab the ones they shoot at us; I can't make any more until we get out of the tree."

She hefted her own bow and took aim. They'd both been trained at archery when they had been in school that year, but neither had particularly excelled. They hadn't been that interested, with Ali focusing on crafting and animal husbandry, and Max focusing on history and architecture like the rest of his family. But they were required to learn how to protect themselves if they ever came across a skeleton, zombie, or creeper.

Twang went the arrow, and the shot flew wide. The skeleton she'd aimed at noticed her then, and fired back. She ducked. "Thanks!" she shouted at it, and grabbed the arrow that had just missed her and lodged in a branch. She fired again. This one struck home, going straight through the skull of a skeleton, making it fall.

"Nice one!" Max shouted, and remembered to raise his own bow.

Draw slow, mash the string into your face, and breathe. That was what his teacher had said—weird advice, he'd thought at the time. But whenever he didn't do those three things, the arrow went wild, one of them striking a fellow student and sending him to the nurse for a potion, and Max to the office for discipline.

Don't think about that. Think about the arrow. The only thing here is your arrow, and you, and your target.

Ali took down another skeleton. There were three left, and Max had all three of his arrows. He took one, nocked it, and then pulled the string as far back as he could, breathing out slowly and taking aim. *There.* He aimed for the one backlit by the lava flow.

Max let fly the arrow and it sailed straight into the sternum of the skeleton, causing it to fall backward into the lava where it quickly caught fire.

"Two more!" shouted Ali. "I'm out of arrows unless they shoot more up here. It's all on you!"

Max wanted to give a snarky retort, or at least a brave one, but there was no time. One skeleton was drawing its bow, aiming at Max. He quickly nocked another arrow and let it fly, thinking of nothing else except the target.

The arrow went through the eye socket of the skeleton and it went down without loosing its own arrow. Ali whooped, sounding more excited than he'd heard since she'd come to stay with him. One arrow left. He grinned and took aim at the last one.

This skeleton wasn't aiming at them. It was focused on something on the ground. Max and Alison might as well not even be there. He tensed, the string taut, and prepared to take the last one down and brag about it at dinner. He already knew what he was going to say.

"MAX! WHAT IN THE OVERWORLD ARE YOU DOING?"

Mom had come home.

The last arrow went wild, lodging into the hill where they had unleashed everything.

The fury of Max's mother eclipsed the lava and the skeletons. With a howl of rage, she grabbed a shovel off Francine's pack and swung with all her might, caving in the last skeleton's skull. It went down with a clatter.

She ordered Alison and Max down from the tree and checked them both for injuries, her inspection getting rougher as she became convinced they were unharmed.

Satisfied, she stood back and held out her hands. "Bows," she commanded. They handed them over without complaint. Max glanced over at Alison; her eyes were wide with fear, and he wondered if his looked the same. "Picks!" his mom said, and he reluctantly pulled his out and handed it over. He'd barely used it at all, and now it was gone. Just in case they had any other tools in there, Max's mom went through their packs. She confiscated their shovels, their torches, everything they'd mined, and the wood Alison had gathered while in the tree.

"Where did you get these tools?" she demanded. The kids looked at each other, Alison shaking her head slightly at Max. He had to lie.

He shrugged and said the first thing that came into his head. "We found them. In the woods."

"In an abandoned cabin," Alison added when Max's mom shot them a skeptical look.

He winced immediately. He wished she hadn't said that. His mother knew someone who had recently abandoned a cabin, and she would not be happy if she thought Max had been exploring around there.

Max's mom gasped and looked back and forth between them, and Alison actually took a step back from her.

"Not that cabin, Mom," Max said, ignoring a confused glance from Alison. "Just one near Ali's sheep pen."

Max's mom passed a hand over her face, rubbing her forehead, and sighed, looking very tired. "Go inside. Max's room, both of you. Alison, I don't want you back in your tower until I have searched it for any other tools."

Would she find the door Alison had crafted? Max shared a panicked look with Alison. Mom was a builder; she might find it difficult to count the number of sheep milling about, or catch an escaped animal, but architecture she knew. All would be lost if she found that door into their secret workshop.

They gave her a quick nod and ran inside the house.

Alison and Max stood at the window and watched Max's mom place several torches in the garden and get to work digging a trench to stop the sluggish flow of lava. "This isn't good, and it's going to get worse when she finds our workshop," Max said.

"I'll be back," Alison whispered, and then she raced out of the room.

Max stayed at his window, hoping Alison would be fast, whatever she was doing. You didn't want to disobey your mom when you were already being punished for disobeying. That just led to a cycle of punishment that would keep him in his room until he was thirty.

He watched his mother work, feeling a sharp mix of resentment that she had taken everything away, and guilt that he'd definitely given her a good reason to do so.

"Blocked the door up," Ali gasped, tumbling back into his room. "She probably won't find it unless she thinks to dig into the wall."

"She's an *architect*," Max said, realizing their role reversal as Alison said the ridiculous thing and he had to soberly point out the obvious. "You think I haven't tried to hide things in walls before?"

"So, what, we just wait for your mom to kick us out?" Alison asked, joining him at the window. The trench had lengthened as the sun sank, and mobs started to groan from the perimeter of the light. Max's mom didn't look concerned at all, and Max knew if anything was stupid enough to attack her right now, it would get the business end of her anger.

"We wait for something, but I don't know what," he said. "I've never seen her this mad. At least when I almost drowned she was worried about me. Now she's just mad. Maybe I should have let one of the skeletons hit me."

Alison glared at him, and Max was relieved that he was back to his usual role of saying the weird thing.

"I guess we can't do anything until she tells us what our punishment is," Alison said.

"You're such a rules captive," he said, flopping down on his bed. "Follow all the rules, just like one of your own sheep."

She stared stonily at him. "Clearly you don't know sheep. They don't listen to anyone but the bellwether. Certainly not the shepherd."

"What's a bellwether?" he asked, frowning.

"The one sheep all the other sheep follow. Usually the oldest ewe."

"Oh," he said. "How does a sheep rebel against the bellwether?"

"I'm not getting into this," she said impatiently. "We can't rebel until we know what to rebel against. You might decide to run away because you think she's going to kick you out, when all she was going to do is make you replant the pumpkins."

"You don't know her like I do," he grumbled.

"I know." She looked out the window again. "She's getting tired. We should help her."

"You really think that would help us?" he asked.

"I didn't say help *us*, I said help *her*." She sighed. "But you're right. That would probably cause more harm than good."

"Believe me, right now she just needs to cool off," Max said, staring at the ceiling.

The light in the room changed as the sun went down. "It's too dark," Alison reported. "She's coming in. Let's go see what we're up against."

Alison turned toward the door, taking a few steps before stopping. "Oh, and if I *were* a sheep," she added, "I'd be the bellwether."

. . .

Max's mom was in a strangely good mood when she got into the house. She whistled as she put away the tools, and then hummed as she did a quick search of Alison's rooms. She completely missed their secret workshop.

They had charred pumpkin pie for dinner. Alison and Max sat, staring at the person who really looked like Max's mom, but couldn't possibly be her because she wasn't crying about his safety or shouting at them for their stupid mistakes. She merely had a conversation with them, or had half a conversation while they sat, eyes wide, waiting for the punishment to fall.

"When I was young," she said, "I was chopping up a tree to collect wood, and set loose a bunch of spiders." She paused to take another bite of her pie before continuing. "They fell on my head, bounced off, skittered all around, a few bit me." She chuckled. "I was so scared I screamed." She looked them each in the eyes so they understood the weight of her words. "I was the star apprentice architect. Screaming about a few spiders." She took a deep breath. "So, I ended up squashing them with my shovel to save face. I just tore into them, waving the shovel around, smashing anything that moved. I may have caused more harm than intended, just by not wanting to look stupid. Made a huge mess, but the school quartermaster was really happy to get a bunch of silk to make bows."

"Um," Max said.

"That's . . . nice?" Alison said.

"Today you both thought quickly on your feet. You protected yourselves. Mangling the tree was quick thinking, Max, and Alison, your bows were well made and probably saved you—and me, come to think of it. I'm proud of you, is what I'm trying to say," she said. She took another bite of pie. "I'm furious, don't get me wrong. I don't know what made you decide to tunnel into the hill, and I don't know where you got these tools. I'm taking them along with any others I find. Tomorrow you'll clear the lava out of the garden, re-till the ground, and plant new pumpkins."

Max deflated. He'd actually thought his mom's uncharacteristic good mood meant he'd be off the hook.

Alison cleared her throat. "The cavern that I found in the hill. What if it spawns more skeletons? The hill is still open."

"Well, once you carry enough water from the cove to the garden to cool off the lava, you will have enough cobblestone to plug the hole in the hill, won't you?" his mom said conversationally.

Max thought about going back and forth, carrying water, and then mining out the cobblestone, and groaned. "Hey, Mom, I thought you wanted me to stay away from water," he said, raising his eyebrows.

"Well, that was before you had an adventure with lava and skeletons," she said pleasantly. "I'm sure a bucket of water won't hurt you."

Max winced. He couldn't really argue with that. He was oddly happy that, even in the wake of being grounded, losing his tools, and rebuilding the pumpkin patch, his mom seemed to have lost her severe freak-out when it came to his safety. Regarding water, anyway. Her eyes had a wild look in them still, but she had acknowledged that this was not the same danger he'd faced in the water.

That had been an entirely different situation. He maybe could mention water around her, and maybe she'd even laugh about the lava and skeletons sometime in the future, but if she knew what he had hidden inside their secret workshop, she'd probably be much, much angrier.

Even Alison didn't know what he'd hidden within a wall cavity of their workshop. But Max knew he'd have to tell her sooner or later.

For now, it would be best to move it from the workshop altogether. As for telling Ali, he decided on "later."

We can't do this anymore.

Alison lay on her bed, watching the moon through the skylight as it floated across the sky. She couldn't risk losing the only home she had left.

Granted, Max's mom hadn't threatened to kick her out, but Alison didn't know how many chances they had to push her limits.

But even as she lay there trying to convince herself not to break the rules anymore, she still missed crafting and tried to justify how she could keep making tools without getting in trouble. Even if they weren't allowed to dig through the hill anymore, Max's mom hadn't said Alison couldn't work on her crafting skills.

She tried to envision how it would work: She could take her tools to the village and sell them for materials. Then she could use those materials to make better tools. And sell them to get materials to make more tools to sell, to get more materials . . .

A frustrated sigh left her lips. She loved crafting, but it was empty if you didn't do anything with the tools you made. Someday she wanted to make even better things: armor and weapons, mainly. But she would need a lot of materials for that. And the easiest way to get materials was to mine.

A fat spider fell on her skylight and skittered away. Startled for a moment, she laughed, thinking about Max's mom. *She said my weapon crafting was good, that my bows saved us all from danger,* Alison thought. *She said she was proud of us.*

Alison decided then that if skeletons and lava couldn't stop them, nothing could. She was good at crafting—Max's mom had said so!—and she wanted to keep improving her skills, to take them even further and start making the weapons and armor that she'd always dreamed of, so that she could protect the people she loved.

With visions of legendary weapons and epic armor forming in her mind, she got out of bed and crept down the tower stairs. The door to the workshop was ajar, and her heart gave a painful lurch of fear, but the only person inside was Max. He was crouched over a chest and looked to be inventorying their remaining supplies.

He glanced up when she walked in. "Took you long enough. Where have you been?"

"In bed, where you should be," she said, fully aware she was scolding him for doing exactly what she had come here to do. "I couldn't sleep."

"Me neither. Man, was she mad!"

"She had every right to be, Max." Alison chewed on her lower lip, thinking. "That's why we have to go back in when she can't catch us."

His eyebrows rose in surprise. "Really? I figured you'd want to keep following the rules and give up."

She thought about telling him her goal, but she suddenly felt silly and didn't want to say it out loud. So she just shrugged.

He didn't need much encouragement. "I figure we have enough wood and metal here for you to make some more tools, and we can start excavating at night," Max said. "Since Mom will keep a close eye on us during the day."

"When will we sleep?"

He shrugged. "I dunno, but you're not sleeping now, are you?"

He had a point. She crafted some new tools, got some torches, and they went into the hill to get back to work.

The real tragedy of it all was that their next "incident" wasn't nearly as bad as flooding the farm with lava and skeletons. It was a minor mistake, really.

They'd misread Alison's map. When they found a cave, Max went in to check for mobs while Alison tried to update the map. The cave was massive, at least twenty blocks deep at its deepest level. They'd have to carve in some steps to get around, but it wouldn't be a problem.

But Max always wanted to see what was on the other side, so he insisted on carving out an exit once they'd decided the cave was safe. Alison stared at the map, puzzled, then recognized their mistake too late: they were much closer to the surface than they had originally realized. They broke through and sunlight streamed in.

And after the sunlight, the sheep streamed in.

They had broken through the base of the hill straight into a ranch. Alison recognized it immediately; it belonged to Mr. Hatch, her family's neighbor. She could see his sheep pens, and beyond that, her own sheep pen that he had so graciously offered to help watch for her. This is all she saw, however, before the frightened sheep did the thing that frightened sheep always did.

First, startled by the sudden appearance of two humans popping out of the hill, they ran in the opposite direction. Fuzzy black and white tails waved at Alison as they scrambled for safety. Then, of course, they hit their pen's fence. Unsure of where to run, they ran along the fence looking for a way out. Which eventually brought them back toward Alison and Max, standing stupidly in the mouth of the exit they'd just created.

Alison stepped aside quickly as they neared, but Max stayed in front of the hole.

"Get out of the way!" she shouted.

"We can't let them into the cave, they'll fall and we'll never find them!" Max said, spreading his arms.

"But they will run you over!" Alison said, grabbing his arm.

He shook her off. "Sheep like me."

Alison faced the choice of whether to stand with her friend and take the fall like he would inevitably do, or jump aside and save herself.

When she remembered that if she didn't save herself, no one would be around to find their sheep-trampled bodies, she jumped at the last minute. Max stood there, one arm outstretched to cover the hole, one arm extended, holding a piece of wheat.

The lead sheep, an old ewe named Belle (because she was the bellwether—Mr. Hatch was about as creative with naming as her father had been) grabbed the wheat from Max right before she pushed past him and they both tumbled into the darkness.

Alison was prepared; she'd already taken out her pickaxe. She rammed it into the granite beside her and held on with one hand, then reached out and grabbed Max's arm with the other. She wasn't strong enough to pull him up by herself, but she held on tight and used his falling momentum to swing him to where he could grab the ledge himself.

Max held on as more sheep tumbled in. Their bleating echoed throughout the cave. Alison anchored a torch to the wall and used both hands to help pull Max up.

"Sheep like you, huh?" Alison asked.

"Shut up," Max said, and looked down. "They look okay . . ." he said doubtfully.

The sheep had only fallen about four blocks. Belle was limping but the others looked fine. Alison guessed they had all fallen on Belle and bounced off. The bigger problems were getting them out of the hole and keeping them from falling into a crevasse Alison had just noticed in the corner of the cave.

"Max, did you check out that hole over there?" she asked, pointing.

Max squinted. "No, I didn't see it until now."

"So, it could have skeletons, or zombies, or creepers."

"It could also have more sheep," Max said defensively.

"Sheep don't come from caves!" Alison said. For someone who claimed to be good with sheep, he definitely didn't know a lot about the silly creatures.

Belle had started bleating more forcefully, her panic rising. The other sheep milled around her, taking their cues from her and adding their own panic to the mix. The echoes in the cave only made it worse.

"We need to get them out of here before Mr. Hatch finds us," Alison said. "Come on, let's build some stairs for them."

They didn't have the time or the resources to make actual stairs, so they had to make do with staggered blocks they hoped the sheep would walk up. Their rudimentary "stairs" were two blocks wide, making a steep walkway. Unfortunately, it wasn't as simple as just asking the sheep to hop up the stairs and back to their pen. The animals were already terrified, and ran from Max and Alison. When they tried to herd the sheep onto the steps, they clustered underneath instead.

"Do you have any more wheat?" Alison asked, exasperated.

"None," Max said.

"All right. Keep them away from that hole; I'm going home to get some wheat. I'll be right back."

Alison reached the top of their stairs and jumped into the pen, where she ran straight into a sturdy body. She looked up, dreading the worst.

"Um. Hi, Mr. Hatch. We found your sheep."

Max regretted messing with Alison's map. She needed another win, another way to feel useful, and it shouldn't involve really dangerous things. So he'd just "altered" the map to make them come out at Mr. Hatch's ranch. She could be a hero saving the sheep, and get some confidence back.

But everything had gone wrong, and Alison became a *real* hero when she'd saved him from falling backward into a cave and being buried under sheep.

Max's mom was taking no prisoners now. This situation wasn't nearly as bad as dumping lava and skeletons into the garden, but apparently any mistake you make after lava and skeletons is a very bad mistake, Max thought bitterly.

Luckily, after their last adventure, he had thought to remove his secret from the hiding place in the workshop. Since he was in charge of repairing the garden, he had buried it underneath some pumpkins he'd planted.

That turned out to be a brilliant idea, since this time Max's mom found the workshop. She took their tools, their workbench, their furnace, and began methodically tearing down Alison's tower, block by block.

Alison had asked tearfully if she was being kicked out, and Max's mom stopped raging and said calmly, "Of course not, dear. Very little could make me that angry. You will sleep in Max's room for now."

She went back to work tearing down the tower.

"My room is pretty small, Mom," Max ventured. "Why don't we both move into the tower?"

His mom fixed him with such a glare that he stopped talking.

True to her word, she put a bed in Max's bedroom opposite his own, and then began building a wall down the center of the room. She put a door in her own bedroom wall so Alison could get in and out—and so Alison couldn't sneak around at night without going past her.

"Be good for a week," she said through the open door as Max sat on his bed, "and I'll give you two a window to talk through. Be good for a month and you get a door. Show me you're trustworthy for a year and the wall will go away. Two years and I might rebuild the tower."

A year. Two years. So much could happen in that time. He might die of boredom. But as he flopped back onto his bed, he thought that he'd learned his lesson: Mom was not on board with mining behind the house.

He caught Alison at the breakfast table the next morning tapping her fingers, and he realized she was counting blocks in her head. His mom was at the furnace, cooking breakfast, her back to them.

"What are you planning on doing? You're not going in there again, are you?" he whispered.

"I have to," she said.

"You'll get us thrown into a cage! Just wait a while to let her cool down. What's so important that you're getting right back down to making her mad?"

Alison's face flushed. "I'm making armor. I want to make a set of really, really good armor."

"What?" Max thought the goal was a cool one, but not enough to endanger them and risk his mother's wrath. "Why do you *have* to do that? Why is it so important? Is it for you?"

She shook her head, and he was shocked to see her eyes fill with tears. He gave a panicked look at his mom's back, and then leaned closer. "What did I say? What's wrong?"

"It's for her."

"For who?" Max asked, frowning.

Alison glanced at his mom. "Her." A tear dripped down her face. "I can't lose another parent, Max. I owe her everything. I want her to be safe when she's traveling around all alone. If I get better at crafting I can give her a set of armor to wear when she goes into town, and that can thank her for taking care of me."

Max wanted to take her hand and comfort her. He wanted to shout at her that he was fairly certain his mom would rather Alison just be a regular safe kid and not endanger her life to protect his mom from an imagined threat. He wanted to sit back and just be confused that *this*, this weird thing, was driving his rules-abiding friend into a life of disobedience. And he realized that they had more in common than he'd thought.

What he did do was pass her his napkin so she could wipe her tears. His mom turned around and brought a plate of eggs to the table.

"Alison, what's wrong?" she asked, spying Alison wiping her eyes.

"The thing that's usually wrong," she said, smiling slightly. "Sometimes it just hits me."

Max's mom leaned over and hugged her, which only made her cry harder.

Alison was strangely quiet for the next few weeks of their punishment, nearly back to how she was when she first moved in, grief-stricken and alone. Max wished he could talk to her privately, but his mom kept one of them with her at all times. She took Alison with her to help retrieve Mr. Hatch's sheep and to fix the holes in his farm.

She took Max with her to the village, leaving Alison and Francine at home and making him carry her pack (meaning he couldn't carry his own). He got to see his dad and the building project he was working on, but this time around he found that visiting with Dad wasn't a treat, since he was even angrier than Mom had been.

He asked Alison if she had been mining during these times alone, but she shook her head.

Their punishment included Alison helping Max's mom plan the details of her upcoming projects, while Max grudgingly helped his mom with her designs.

They were busy, that was for sure, but they were also miserable.

After one week, true to her word, Max's mom came in with a pickaxe—one of Alison's fine iron ones, Max noticed—and knocked a hole in the wall between them. She left the mess for them to clean up, but they finally were allowed to talk in private.

"I've got an idea," Max said, standing by the window and looking through to Alison lying with her back to him on the bed.

"What is it?" she said flatly, rolling over and staring at the ceiling. "I need to get back to making things. I just . . . need to."

"I think she'll be okay, Ali. You remember how she took care of that skeleton?"

"What's your idea?" she asked, ignoring him. "Does it include waiting till she stops being mad?"

"Eh, she's already over it," he said, waving off the concern. He was too excited to worry about anything right now. "I have something I want to show you."

Alison tucked her knees to her chin, rolling herself into a tiny ball. "No, Max. She is definitely not over it. She won't forget what we did to her garden, and the next time we mess up, she will remember the sheep *and* the garden. We have to be more careful."

"You're right, there. But I'm not talking about mining, or even crafting," he said. He hesitated a moment, then slid a book into the window, resting it in the cavity of the missing block. "I'm talking about so much more."

That, at least, got her attention.

Max passed his precious find through the window reverently, as if it were breakable. The journal was bound in cracked brown leather. A rough circle with two dots in the center was burned into the cover, and the whole thing looked handmade. Alison grabbed it and opened it to a random page: it was filled with scribbles having to do with potion recipes the author had experimented with.

"Where did you get this?" she asked, running her finger down the page and squinting at some crossed-out parts.

"I found it in a cabin," he said. "Remember when you asked where I got the obsidian to fix your sheep pen?" She nodded, still studying the messy writing. "The obsidian wasn't the only thing I found."

She flipped another page carefully. "There's a lot crossed out here. Or just missing."

"I figure it's a book of experiments—some of them didn't work."

Alison flipped back to the recipe for the potion of water breathing. "See, this one says it's for water breathing, but the recipe listed here isn't one I've ever seen before. I don't know all the uses for fermented spider eyes, but I do know they aren't used for a lot of beneficial spells or potions."

Max leaned as far as he could through the hole in the wall, frowning. "I didn't know that."

She raised an eyebrow. "Max, that was in our basic potions class. How can you be interested in enchanting and brewing and not know that?"

"That was a long time ago, and it was really boring," he said defensively. "And besides, the book still has a lot of cool stuff in it regardless. Keep reading."

"Okay, so there are some potions in here that look like they work. And some detailed enchanting information. Oh, this is good." Max made himself be quiet while she read, only bouncing slightly as he waited. He was hoping she would find the best part before he had to point it out, but she stayed on an enchanting page, which talked about weapons and armor. "Max, do you realize that with this book, I could make armor and you could enchant it? We could enchant weapons!" Her voice was starting to get that curious excitement that he knew always came before she agreed to one of his schemes.

"I know!" he said. "But keep looking. It gets better."

"What is better than an enchanted sword?" she asked, but kept turning the pages. "An enchanted helmet," she muttered to herself as she read.

Max waited for her to get closer to the back of the book to find the sketch. The earlier pages had been sloppy and haphazard, but this page looked like an entirely different person had written it. The script was small, precise, with clear measurements and a detailed sketch of a large rectangle surrounded by cubes of obsidian. In the center of the rectangle was a flaming bowl. The rectangle had been filled in with swirls; you couldn't see beyond the structure, even though it didn't look like it contained any blocks.

Below the sketch were three words.

She looked up at Max. "Is this for real?"

"There is only one way to find out!" he said, grinning widely.

Alison looked back down at the book and ran her finger over the words.

PORTAL TO NETHER

CHAPTER 5

A STICK, A PICKAXE, AND ADVENTURE

What Max and Alison knew about the Nether:

According to school, it was a forbidden, mysterious place, and the kids weren't really sure why it was so secret since no one would tell them how to get there in the first place.

According to Max's parents, it was a myth that deranged adventurers told as they wandered through town.

According to Alison's Grandma Dia, it was a word you didn't say unless you wanted a very long lecture about spreading falsehoods, and about the price of not being prepared, and she would talk so long that Alison would wonder only much later why you needed to be prepared to visit a place that wasn't real.

And according to every reference book they could find, it was a chapter that was often torn out, but sometimes not removed from the table of contents.

And, on the topic of everyday word usage, Alison had once wondered: If they lived in the *Over*world, what exactly was it *over*, anyway?

So, what they figured out was: It was definitely a place. It was definitely dangerous. And it was hard to get to—or at least hard to figure out how to get to.

Thus Max, of course, thought that they definitely had to go.

Alison insisted on waiting another week—until Max's mom had officially allowed them to go out of the house together—before they snuck out again. She wouldn't bend on this, and Max couldn't go without her; he had little skill with crafting and he'd need her help with some repairs to things in the cabin. The fact that she wouldn't just break the rules right away annoyed him to a level he hadn't known she could achieve.

He dealt with his feelings by avoiding her for the last few days of their punishment. This wasn't hard because his mom still kept them busy and apart.

Alison politely waited for him to cool off. She knew he'd come back around; he just wanted the adventure *right now*. Secretly, Alison couldn't blame him, but she just couldn't afford to push Max's mom any further. The chore of coaxing (and in some cases lifting and carrying) Mr. Hatch's sheep from the cave had been enough of a pain to cause her to tread lightly in their next excursion.

The problem was, they had gotten quite good at helping Max's mom. Now she was using their assistance more for the actual benefit rather than as a punishment. And when she wasn't super angry with them, Max's mom was actually okay to be around. Alison still wanted to go and see the cabin where Max had found the journal, but the heavy work they were doing was wearing her out.

"You two have done a good job," Max's mom said over dinner

one night. "I'm lifting the ban on going outside. But don't mess up again."

Alison nodded gratefully. But she remembered her promise, and when she and Max were back in their room, she put her face up to the hole between them and said, "She's not going to give us any free time during the day. Let's go tonight."

Surprisingly, Max was too tired. He was still grubby from all the work he'd done in the garden and was lying on his back, nearly asleep.

"Already? I thought you'd want to wait a few days," he moaned.

"Are you kidding me?" she asked. "You're the one who was in such a hurry earlier—"

He laughed and sat up, his eager energy showing again. "Completely kidding," he said. "Let's go."

Max said he'd found the journal in an abandoned cabin in the woods a ways from his house. They needed to go back there, because he hadn't explored half of the secrets it held. Luckily, Max's mom had sent Alison to the shed to fetch a tool earlier that day, and Alison had used the crafting table within to make a quick, basic pickaxe.

She quietly broke through the bedroom wall separating them, and they were both able to leave by Max's door.

They carried torches as they walked through the woods. The only weapons they had were a stick and the wooden pickaxe, and Alison asked if they should find some sort of real weapon or armor.

"We'll be fine with the torches. I know this area pretty well, I mapped it before the accident, when I had free time. The path is fairly safe, and the cabin's safe too."

Alison still looked around, eyes wide as she tried to spot any mobs lurking in the trees. But the path to the cabin was clear, and their torches kept any interested creatures away.

The cabin itself was in a shambles. The breath caught in Alison's throat as she realized what it looked like: a creeper attack. She did not like creepers. She took a step back, thought she heard a hissing in the woods, and whirled around—

Nothing there. Her breath was coming fast, and she became light-headed. Max wasn't there. Had he left her like everyone else had? Was she alone? She took in a deep breath and tried to still the panic.

A hand grasped her elbow, and she jerked away violently. It was Max, looking calm and concerned. "I went to put torches everywhere so we're less likely to get bothered," he said, gesturing to the house. It was now lit on all sides by torches. "Are you okay?"

Her eyes felt opened too wide, and she nodded mutely. He turned and walked toward the cabin. "I didn't warn you that it was a mess, sorry about that." He led her to the eastern side, which was completely gone. "I've salvaged and stacked most of the stuff I found here so Mom couldn't confiscate it from me," he said, pointing to blocks of wood and stone. "It's safe to go inside."

More torches glowed from inside, beckoning them with their warmth. Since Max had cleaned up, instead of a wall of rubble there was just a hole. They climbed inside to find some furniture, a bed, a stove, and other simple things one needed to live.

"Wait till you see the basement," he said, noticing her facial expression. Had she looked disappointed?

She didn't know what to think; she was still thinking about her family.

"Whose cabin is this?" Alison finally asked, trying to dampen the fear in her voice.

"It's abandoned, don't worry," he said. "Let me show you downstairs."

He lit a few torches and put them in sconces, starting with the stairway. The basement's full sprawl revealed itself slowly. Alison sucked in a sharp breath as she took in the bookcases, the enchanting tables, the workbenches, crafting tables, furnaces, and chests. The walls featured art of all kinds, both good and terrible (the flower still-life and the landscape with the cove were good; the worst one looked like a close-up painting of an enderman, which seemed like a weird thing to paint). On the end of the basement that had stretched beyond the cabin above, moonlight filtered down from a hidden skylight Max had found in the forest floor and cleaned.

"This has to belong to someone," Alison whispered. "No one would leave all this just lying around."

"Well, someone did," Max said, "And I have—" He stopped speaking when Alison rushed past him to the crates and opened one.

"It's full of metal!" she cried. "Iron and gold and even a little bit of diamond!"

Another chest held tools, picks and shovels and axes of quality materials Max knew that Alison had never seen before. Many of them were poorly treated and needed fixing, but they were still nicer than most.

She finally found what she was looking for in the third chest. She opened it up and gasped. "Whoever lived here was a crafter." Alison pulled out a sword and held it up to Max. It was gold, and well made.

"Wait, don't just go running around grabbing stuff—" he began, but she kept searching.

"And obviously a crafter lived here," he added, indicating all of the crafting benches. "I figured we would need a safe place for you to make things and me to"—he lowered his voice even though they were underground and far from any other living being— "run some experiments."

Alison's emotions ran from hopeful to skeptical. "Thanks, but I still don't understand who would leave all this stuff. Even if they moved because their cabin blew up."

Max took a deep breath. He looked strangely nervous, but forged on with his next comment. "I know why the Enchanter isn't here. Let me show you."

Alison couldn't speak.

Max bounced slightly beside her, eager for her response, but she couldn't come up with any words at all.

A clearing lay a ways behind the cabin, the perimeter lit by Max's torches. While the house was a shambles, the clearing was pristine, with the trees trimmed back, torches casting gentle light on the grass, and everything drawing the eye to the object in the center. A large black rectangle stood there, obsidian gleaming in the torchlight. She paused for a moment, and Max wondered if she would yell at him, but then she stepped forward and inspected the area. Sitting on the edge of the clearing was a neat stack of more obsidian, just in case the Enchanter had wanted to make the doorway even bigger.

Because that's what it was. A doorway. And Max wanted to go through.

On top of the stack of obsidian, Alison fingered the flint, steel, and shiny pickaxe sitting there.

She gazed up at the structure. It was at least eight blocks high and four wide. "This used so much obsidian," she whispered. "Where did it all come from?"

Max glanced around. There was no obvious source of lava or water within sight, so someone had to have mined pretty deep to get the obsidian—or they'd created it and carted it here.

"That's not—that isn't what I think it is, is it?" she said.

"It's a real portal to the Nether! It exists! And I think the author of the journal is there!" Max said, unable to contain his glee any longer.

"You took the obsidian from the Enchanter's stash and used it to fix the sheep pen." It wasn't a question. She sounded baffled, like she had to say the words out loud to make sure they were real.

He shrugged, annoyed she hadn't taken his conversational lead to the next logical thought. "I figured it would work. And get you interested. But Ali, you know what this means."

She looked sideways at him. "No," she said, as if she knew what he was getting at, but refused to say it.

"Yeah, you do," he said. "We have the journal and the supplies, everything we need. We can go through the portal!"

"Are you insane?" she yelled. "We're kids! We can't even handle rampaging sheep! What makes you think that we could, first, find the Enchanter, and second, survive whatever is on the other side?"

Max pointed back toward the cabin. "Because you're going to craft us some weapons and armor, and I'm going to enchant them. Then we're going to the Nether to rescue the Enchanter."

CHAPTER 6

THE DIFFERENCE BETWEEN
LIGHTNING AND LIGHTENING

Alison demanded time to think about it. They returned to Max's house, sneaking in and rebuilding the wall in the bedroom so Max's mom would be none the wiser. Alison spent a distracted day doing odd jobs around the house and garden, and then a sleepless night watching the moon wander the sky while she thought, listening to Max's slow breathing through the window in the wall.

All she'd wanted to do was become a better crafter and make Max's mom some armor to protect her. And then some for his dad, too, even though he currently lived in the village. And sure, she didn't know how she would present the armor to them without admitting she and Max had been crafting a lot more than his parents knew about, but that was a problem for another sleepless night. The issue keeping her up now was how she would give armor to Max, because Alison wanted to protect him, too.

But I want to make armor for him so he'll be safe, not so he can do something as absurd as go through the nether portal, she thought. *How can I protect him if he's just going to use the armor to go after the Enchanter?*

She frowned, feeling stuck, before she was hit by the thought that Max would go no matter what. She'd recognized that determined look in his eyes when he said they were going to the Nether; it meant he'd already decided to throw caution to the wind.

Alison had spent her life being careful. What's more careful than tending sheep and making clothes out of their garish wool? She had never mined before coming to live with Max, never fought skeletons, never entered abandoned cabins in the woods.

She could continue being careful. Safe. She could refuse Max's request to go to the Nether, and return to helping Max's mom. Maybe she could teach Alison architecture. She might even be allowed to craft another workbench eventually, provided she and Max didn't immediately start using the tools for wild and exciting purposes.

They could cut down trees, for example. There was nothing more exciting than cutting down trees . . .

She rolled over, going over the recipes she knew for armor and weapons. She fell asleep dreaming of diamond equipment and glimmering portals.

"If we're doing this, we're going to make sure we know what we're getting into," Alison said, after her ears stopped ringing from Max's whoop of joy. His mom had left them alone for a short trip to Mr. Hatch's ranch to check on his sheep—Belle was still limping, last they'd heard—and Alison was very aware that this was a test of their obedience. Max dragged out the old journal and they started going through it.

The first several pages held food recipes. Some of them had the standard recipes for mutton and pork chops, but others had recipes using mushrooms and flowers, or bat meat scorched by lava.

"Have you tried this one?" she asked, pointing to a recipe for candied mushrooms.

"No, I can't cook," he said.

"And you want to be an enchanter," she said, rubbing her forehead. "All right, has your mom tried to make them?"

"No, I can't let her see the journal. She'd take it away from me!" he said.

"There are a lot of things in here I don't remember seeing in school," she said, flipping another page. "I don't know if we should trust this 'Enchanter,' as you call them."

"But the portal is real!" he protested. "We know that's right."

"You want to risk our lives based on that?" she asked, glaring at him. She flipped another page. There were some empty pages, possibly leaving room to put more recipes, and then there was a section seemingly dedicated to structures.

The drawings here were lovingly detailed, shaded, and contained block-by-block measurements.

Why didn't Max call this author "the Builder"? Whoever had written this was clearly a master of architecture. The first page of the section had plans for a complicated mining system with conveyor belts and steps and ladders. Another detailed a tunnel system with reinforced walls, for delving deep in a safer manner than Alison and Max had done. Then they got more fantastic: a floating, flaming beacon high in the sky above the tree line. An underwater mansion (with a note that, before construction, the builder should check the underwater breathing recipes and plans on a later page), complete with pens to hold squid. It left out the fact that squid could just swim up and over the fences, but the drawing was nice, with obedient squid sitting placidly in their pens. A great structure that had mining rails that rose and fell like hills, and small mining cars linked together to zip around the tracks. It didn't look like it had much of a purpose, but it did look like fun.

Once she got out of the construction section, the handwriting changed back to scrawling writing, the author getting frustrated at times, with angry cross-outs of whole sections. Alison noticed Max's handwriting in the margins, sometimes trying to puzzle out what had been originally written there, sometimes actually offering encouragement, as if his words could go back in time and support the frustrated author.

She wondered about Max's investment in this. He'd always shown a passing interest in enchanting; at school he thought it was neat, but not neat enough to study.

Then again, it was hard being excited about a subject with a teacher who demanded their students be cautious at every turn, and who focused only on minor enchantments, and even then *only* after several hours on the history of enchanting, and doing it after lunch when everyone was sleepy. Now they had a mysterious, handwritten journal, an abandoned cabin, and all the tools they needed to basically try anything they wanted. Who *wouldn't* want to explore enchanting?

Alison, for one. She was much more interested in the proper construction of a shiny golden helmet than in magicking it up to handle underwater breathing. She thought about how much gold she had seen in the chests at the cabin, and her hands started clenching and unclenching, eager to start working.

She took a deep breath and patiently started reading the journal again. Nearer to the end, she found more and more heavily scratched-out recipes and methods, many with the word *FAIL-URE* scrawled over the pages. Some were ripped. Alison thought for a moment and decided she had a little work to do.

Max's mom was hesitant to let them do anything together, but she had relaxed her rules to allow them to do things alone, and she always had sympathy whenever Alison wanted to go home to retrieve something or check on her sheep. For now, due to Max's mom's insistence, Mr. Hatch was taking care of Alison's sheep since she had been grounded.

Alison felt Mr. Hatch had gotten the bad end of the deal: she and Max had made a hole in the man's farm, made his sheep fall into the hole, and he'd had to work hard to get the sheep out of the hole—and Mr. Hatch's reward for this suffering was to add Alison's brightly colored, garish sheep to his own proper black-and-white flock. But he had agreed, because he'd taken pity on Alison since the accident.

But Alison still wanted to check on the sheep, even though they had moved to Mr. Hatch's ranch. They were happily milling around with the black-and-white sheep, but she could tell Apple and Lil' Prince were itching to get out and find some water and possibly a squid to befriend.

She scratched Apple behind her ears. "Someday you'll get back out there. But I can't take you today." The sheep looked at her as if she didn't trust Alison, but she couldn't do anything more to convince the animal, so she just shrugged.

She went on to the ruin that was her house, her heart growing heavy as she approached it. No one had been by to clear the land of the great hole, and the tree was still a wreck. She felt even worse when she realized that cleaning it up was her job, as the only person left in her family. Whom was she expecting to take care of things?

The one change she had made was adding a new ladder so she could get to the few rooms that remained intact, and she climbed that and entered her mother's study.

The desk still stood there, alongside a painting of poppies and a chest. Alison hadn't gone through things since leaving, and she knew she didn't have time now, but she figured she would take back everything she could carry in addition to what she was there for.

She searched her mother's desk and found what she needed quickly: a mostly blank book. Her mother had used it much like the Enchanter had done, writing down various patterns for different color combinations and styles of banners, followed by an animal husbandry page listing the sheep that had been bred together to maximize color purity and minimize inbreeding. But apart from those ten pages, the book was completely blank.

She took a couple of her mother's other books, some family pictures, and as much of her mother's stash of wool as she could carry. She climbed down the ladder and saw Mr. Hatch with the sheep. She waved at him, but was too embarrassed to say hello and make small talk. But at least she was on the right side of his ranch this time.

Max was downright offended that she wanted to rewrite the journal in a clean book. "I've already puzzled out most of the things. My notes are right," he said, crossing his arms.

"I didn't say they weren't," Alison said. "It's simply neater to get it rewritten. I'm willing to write down your added notes, but the journal is torn, water-stained, burned, with a lot crossed out."

"I know! That's what makes it amazing!" he said.

"Look, I just want to make my own notes," she said. "You can keep working from the messy journal if you have to."

"I've figured out lots of stuff," he said, hunching over the journal as if she were going to take it away from him. "Why can't we just go on through?"

"We need to test some things before we just run through," she said. "Transcribing the notes won't hurt the journal in any way, Max."

Later that night, Max paced the length of the cabin's basement, glaring at Alison as she wrote another "failed experiment" down in her blank book.

"You can stop looking at me like that," she said patiently. "It's not my fault the experiment failed."

On the brewing stand in front of them, the failed remains of a recipe continued to release tendrils of smoke into the air, despite the bucket of water Max had thrown at it. Alison had tried the recipe to make a potion of swiftness and it had failed so spectacularly that the bottle they'd used melted, leaving a twisted and ruined memory of glass on the workbench.

"Maybe you did something wrong," he said.

"Maybe you shouldn't put fermented spider eyes in beneficial potions," she said.

She had painstakingly arrived at a recipe list—the ones that worked (both potions of healing and regeneration included, thank goodness) and the ones that didn't: candied mushrooms, a potion that claimed to turn everything you touched green for one hour, and a potion that was supposed to let a human grow feathers. Luckily, that was the one that exploded before Max had a chance to drink it. Alison had a feeling it wouldn't have gone so well.

She checked in the furnace; the gold was almost done smelting.

"I'm getting worried," Alison said. "If the Enchanter couldn't make some of these basic recipes work, then why do you think their portal to the Nether was a success? Why do you think they even went through?"

"Because we saw it!" he said, pointing at the wall, beyond which was the waiting portal. "Because who would make a portal and *not* go through?"

"We saw a bunch of obsidian arranged in the *design* of a portal. We have no idea if it worked, or if anyone even needs rescuing."

"I'm still going to try these recipes, whether you're with me or not," he said stubbornly. "What about this one? You make me a pair of boots, and I will try to fly with them."

She looked over his shoulder. He was pointing to a recipe with several annotations and crossed-out words, but essentially the enchantment was supposed to make the wearer light and able to jump far.

"That seems a dangerous one to try," she said doubtfully.

"No, no, it'll be fine. What about those boots?" he asked, pointing to the wall where Alison had been neatly lining up her equipment so that he could test enchantments on them. At the end was a simple pair of leather boots.

She sighed. This was what they were here for, like it or not. "Sure, give it a try."

He jumped up, grabbed the boots, and ran to the enchanting table and the bookcase next to it. He pulled a book off the shelf at random and flipped through it, frowning. "This is so much more boring than the journal," he complained.

"Probably more precise, though," she said.

Max rummaged around one of the chests with the magical supplies in it, and set to work, returning to the journal for instructions instead of the enchanting books readily available. He squinted to read some of the crossed-out words.

"Don't you think those words are crossed out for a reason?" she asked, but he shushed her.

She shrugged and retrieved the golden helmet, which shone with such beauty she could do little but stare at it. For the first time she was confident that if they went to the Nether, she might survive it.

A bright flash lit up the other side of the room. "Done!" Max shouted. He waved the boots above his head.

Nothing had exploded. Alison frowned. They hadn't had a lot of wins thus far, but to be fair, this one seemed somewhat promising.

"All right," she said slowly.

"Let's try them out!" Max said, and bounded up the stairs as if he were already wearing them.

When she caught up with him outside, he had climbed halfway up a hill near the cabin. "Don't you think you should try them on flat ground?" she asked, looking down the hill bathed in moonlight.

"Nah," he said, his shoes already off. He tossed them down the hill and pulled the boots on. "Tingly!"

"All right, so you should take a practice jump first—" Alison said, but Max was gone.

He took a leap off the top of the hill with a loud whoop and sailed outward. And for one shining moment Alison thought he might have actually, successfully enchanted something. And then he flipped to where his feet were up and he dangled by the boots, and then he dropped like a stone. His triumphant noises turned to grunts of pain as he pinwheeled down the hill, head over heels, the boots holding his feet high in the air so he could never get his bearings.

"Now will you stop testing things at the tops of hills?" she called. He didn't respond, so she ran down after him.

They were lucky that they remembered how to brew simple health potions, and had made several before trying any of the experiments, for just this situation. Max coughed and opened his eyes after Alison poured the potion down his throat. "Did it work?"

"You knocked yourself out, you tell me," she said, making him drink more. He pushed her hands away and took the bottle himself, downing the rest of the potion with a painful grimace.

"Maybe I should stop taking your advice," he said.

"It's *my* fault?" she asked, incredulous. "Maybe you should stop doing enchanting and alchemy with fermented spider eyes! What is your Enchanter's obsession with spider eyes? I've been praying you run out of them soon because then you might stop making things with them, but I checked, you have like a year's supply of those things!"

"They're useful," he said, rubbing the back of his head.

"For what? Name one good thing you've made with those!" Alison yelled. "It's like your Enchanter found a sale on spider eyes and decided to stock up, and put them in any and all potions!"

He winced as her voice gained volume. "Please don't yell," he moaned, feeling a bump on his forehead that had yet to go away with the effect of the potion.

"We are nowhere near ready to go through a nether portal, Max. We'll get killed!"

"Alison, I can't do it without you," he said. "Just let me try a few things."

"Max, I don't want to die. I don't want you to die. You can't tell me that we won't straight-up land in the middle of a huge mob if we go through that thing. My grandma always told me not to jump anywhere if you don't know where you're going to land. Besides, your Enchanter will probably want to use spider eyes somewhere in the activation."

"No, he doesn't use spider eyes to activate it," Max said. "He was pretty sure they would reinforce an enchanted door, though."

Alison paused. "Wait. How do you know it's a 'he'? I thought you didn't know anything about this person?"

Max drained another potion, probably more slowly than he needed to. "I thought I saw a reference in the journal to being a grandfather or uncle or something," he said, clearing his throat.

Alison had read the journal thoroughly. "I didn't see that."

"It was in one of the crossed-out parts," he said, not looking at her. He sighed. "Look, if I can prove the Enchanter's enchantments are legit, will you consider it?"

"That's a really big 'if,' Max," she said. "That's like an 'if' that's seventeen blocks high."

"I can build that," he said, thinking.

"Whatever. It's getting late. We need to go home," she said, and he nodded. He stood up and immediately fell on his face as his feet rose and tipped him over again. He'd forgotten the botched flying boots.

"Throw those away," Alison said impatiently.

He bent at the waist and pried his foot out of one of the boots.

It righted itself and hovered in the air with an important manner about it, as if it were waiting on another human to trick. Now Max hung by one foot in midair, twitching and trying to get to the other boot.

Alison watched him, trying to hold back laughter. "You really think we can make a portal to the Nether, rescue the Enchanter, and make it back alive? We can't even rescue the mayor from a bathroom, the way we're going."

"Help me!" he said, his midair struggles making him turn in circles.

She crossed her arms with a grin. "Maybe."

They snuck back in, repaired the wall, and went to bed. At least, Alison did. Exhaustion took her into a dreamless sleep immediately. A few hours later she woke up, as usual, with Max's mom cracking open the door between their rooms and calling her name softly. She grunted and sat up. She wouldn't trade her late-night excursions to the secret crafting cabin for anything, but she had to admit that too many hours awake was catching up with her. She groaned and rubbed her face, blinking a few times. She focused on the foot of her bed, where something gleamed steadily at her.

It was the golden helmet she'd made last night, but it was gleaming in a different, definitely magical way. She looked around, but if Max had snuck in he had covered his tracks very well. She checked to make sure Max's mom had closed the door behind her, picked up the helmet, and inspected it. Like Max had said about the enchanted boots, the helmet made her hands tingle slightly as she turned it over and over.

There was no way she would try it on. But clearly Max had

gone back to the cabin. She was torn between being irritated that he'd gone without her, concerned that he'd enchanted alone without a backup, and touched that he had made a present for her.

She'd have to ask him at breakfast what the enchantment was supposed to do, if she could find a way to get rid of Max's mom.

Luckily, his mother was distracted this morning by a new project in town Max's dad needed her help on. "I'm trusting you kids alone today," she warned. "I need to get to work on a new wing of the Silver Mansion."

"Isn't that just what that merchant Mr. Jordan calls his house?" Max asked, frowning.

"Yes," his mom said with a sigh.

"Can we give our house a name? Like 'Flying Fortress' or something?" he asked.

"It doesn't fly. And it's not a fortress," Alison pointed out.

"And Mr. Jordan's house isn't made of silver," Max retorted. "He's just trying to be fancy."

"And he can afford to be," Max's mom reminded him. "He pays us the maximum we charge to make him a house he can be proud to give a ridiculous name to."

"Someday I'll be rich enough to give stupid names to things," Max announced.

"I just want you to live long enough to make it to 'someday,'" his mom said.

Max rolled his eyes. "I haven't almost died in weeks, Mom."

Alison thought about bringing up last night, but he had only bumped his head badly, and besides, if his mom knew about the cabin they might never leave their rooms again. His mom might dig a hole, throw them in, cover them up with dirt, and tell them not to come out until adulthood.

His mom left with a reminder not to leave the house, which Alison and Max promptly did once she was past the clearing.

"Okay, come clean, what did you do to this?" Alison asked, holding the gleaming helmet in her hands. "And why did you go back without me?"

"I wanted to prove to you that the journal is more useful than you think," he said. "I enchanted it so you can see into the future."

Alison frowned, skeptical. "That's impossible. This is one of the failed enchantments, isn't it?"

Max ignored the question. "Go ahead, try it on," he challenged.

She shook her head. "I saw what your boots did to you. And you could have thrown in a spider eye and cursed this for all I know." She thrust it at him. "You do it."

He frowned in mock pain, overplaying his hurt feelings. "Fine. Don't trust me." He took the helmet and carefully placed it over his head. It rested on his forehead and protected about three-quarters of his head, leaving only a small space for his face. Alison held her breath and waited for him to, well, do anything that would indicate the helmet was cursed or otherwise poorly enchanted.

"I see you're very delighted with this gift I've given you!" he said. He lifted the helmet off and grinned at her. "It's totally fine, Ali."

"Fine," she mumbled. "Give it here."

The helmet fit her perfectly, and she took another moment to be proud of her craftsmanship. She would be satisfied to sit in the Enchanter's cabin for the next year, crafting and never touching the enchanting table. She waited a moment, but no insights into the future occurred to her. "I'm not getting anything," she said.

"Really?" he asked. "That's weird. I was so sure."

"Maybe it only works once?" Alison said, unable to deny her disappointment. But if it had worked, and Max had seen her delighted, then why would she be disappointed now?

She lifted it off. "It's a dud. At least you didn't give it any bad effects," she said.

"The enchantment worked," he said, looking hurt. "I know it. I'm just not sure what the effect is."

She had been too harsh, she realized immediately. "Max, look, I believe that you enchanted it." She stared at him until he looked up and met her eyes. "We'll figure it out."

"Nah, don't lie to me. Don't waste my time." He turned from her and started to trudge toward the cabin.

She grabbed him by the shoulder and pulled him around. "Max. If you enchanted it, and it didn't blow up or obviously fail, then it probably worked. We just have to figure out what you did."

"You just said it was a dud," he said.

"What do I know? I don't know enchanting! You do. Do you believe that you succeeded in putting some kind of enchantment on it? Honestly?"

He paused, the angry look leaching from his face. "Yes," he admitted.

"Then we'll figure it out. Together. Okay?"

He nodded once. "Okay. Thanks."

She put the helmet back on her head, but still didn't feel anything different except a slight tingle. As they headed back to the cabin, she realized that she'd been telling the truth. She did trust him to learn enchanting. He was brash and reckless, but he wasn't stupid.

CHAPTER 7

BOOM, SURELY

Max's mom knew something was up.

The sting of the helmet failure passed quickly as Max read more about enchanting from the journal. At home, Max happily made breakfast every morning now, usually getting up before his mom so he could get practice with cooking—to better try the recipes in the book. Alison had shown him how to use the improved furnace and equipment, and his growing brewing and alchemical skills were making his meals actually edible.

His mom was certainly grateful for the help, but he was pretty sure it was written in the Mom Handbook that no mother will simply accept a sudden bout of helpfulness from a kid; something had to be up.

"What has gotten into you?" she asked, eyeing her breakfast muttonchops suspiciously. "Have you drugged me?"

"Mom!" he protested. "Can't a kid do something nice for his mother?"

"No," she said. "It's really unheard of."

"I think what he means is we've caused you enough trouble in the past few weeks," Alison said, biting into her own breakfast. "We figured we'd do something nice." She swallowed. "See? No poison."

Good save, he thought. *Not to mention we don't want you to notice right away how good the tools around the house have gotten.*

Alison had insisted on continuing to improve the tools in the house. She said it was partly for practice, partly because she felt bad deceiving his mom when she'd been so generous. She would offer to cut wood for the furnace so Max could cook dinner; then she'd go out with the old iron axe and come back in with a bunch of wood and a shiny new iron axe. His mom never noticed.

The day he had tried to enchant Alison's helmet, his outlook on the world drastically changed. Max had snuck into the woods after he'd heard Alison was asleep. When she'd lost her temper about the spider eyes, he realized she might be on to something, no matter how much that annoyed him. He thought that maybe the spider eyes could be included in the recipes by the Enchanter for the specific reason that people *wouldn't* follow his recipes. If Max could figure out what kind of ingredient—if any—the spider eyes replaced, then the recipes might work. Once he got that down, and he found the Enchanter's stash of lapis lazuli, from there it would be easy.

Alison had said she would consider going through the portal. Max was getting more confident with his skills, and if she trusted him, then she might help him. He knew the Enchanter was in the Nether, and he was sure that the Enchanter needed help. He may not be able to convince Alison of this, but he knew she wouldn't let him go through alone.

His mom had slowly reduced the terms of their grounding, and he and Alison were actually able to get some real work done during the day now, provided they got their chores finished. They didn't burrow into the hill, chop down any more trees, or accidentally open up holes into any neighbors' farms, so they were almost above suspicion. So long as they followed the rules of getting home by sundown and avoiding any injuries or burns while crafting, they were in the clear.

When they finished sanitizing the pumpkin patch of skeletal remains, they cooled the last of the lava with buckets of water, making loads of cobblestone that then had to be excavated.

"I thought water and lava made obsidian," Max lamented. "But that doesn't seem to be the case."

"I think you have to be at the source of the lava," Alison said.

Max opened his mouth to suggest going back into the cave Alison had found, but when she glared at him, he shut it.

"We could get the blocks from the sheep pen," Alison said as they relaxed, exhausted from hauling the cobblestone out of the garden. "But why do you want to? We don't need extra anyway. The portal is ready."

"But I can't imagine you can ever have too much obsidian. If we got separated from the portal in the Nether, we'd need to build another one! But if we took those blocks, what would fix the holes in the pen?" Max asked.

She looked at him and laughed. "Actual wood, fence segments, gates, you know, proper patches. Not just stacks of highly valuable blocks."

He shrugged. "It worked, didn't it?"

"Keeping them inside the house would work too, but we don't do that either," she countered.

He gave an exaggerated sigh. "All right, let's get the ones from the pen."

"And fix the pen," she reminded him.

"And fix the pen," he agreed.

Unfortunately, the diamond pickaxe was one of the things that they had to keep back at the cabin, lest Max's mom discover it. They couldn't do much with the obsidian blocks that were now patching up the fence.

Mr. Hatch had returned some of the sheep to their pens temporarily, stating that he needed to take his bellwether to get some confidence training, so Lil' Prince and Apple stood at the fence to watch them hopefully, but all the kids managed to do was poke at the heavy blocks with their tools before they gave up.

"The obsidian back at the cabin will have to be enough for you," Alison said, putting her pick away.

"Sorry about the fence," he said. "It seemed like a good idea."

"Well, your obsidian patch worked, but it worked like using a diamond pick to mine cobblestone," she said ruefully. "Let's go."

Back at the cabin, they discovered the Enchanter did have more obsidian in one of his chests. That stash, plus what they could gather from beside the portal, was more than enough to build another portal. While Max did hate the loss of the valuable obsidian blocks back at the pen, he admitted he didn't really need them.

Once Alison had crafted enough equipment, she felt it might be time to at least test the portal. They had their equipment and extra obsidian stashed in a chest next to the portal. Alison gazed up at it. "This portal is *huge*," she said. "Too big for what was needed."

"How can a portal be too big?" Max said, looking at the portal in wonder. "Big or small, it's a door."

"Well, it's a waste of resources, isn't it?" she said. "Obsidian isn't easy to come by, so if you want to get to the Nether, if it exists —"

"It exists," Max interjected.

"*If* it exists, then why not use the bare minimum? Why work to get over twenty-six blocks when you need only fourteen?" She squinted at the plans. "Actually, we'd only need ten. At least, according to your Enchanter, we don't need to fill in the corners here." She pointed to an alternate portal plan drawn in the corner of the page. It looked like a rectangle except that it was missing the four blocks that made up the corners.

"Ten? That's it?" Ten didn't sound very impressive. When Max imagined a nether portal, he imagined a huge gaping door into another world, not something slightly larger than his front door.

"Luckily we have ten blocks," she said. "If you want to wait until we have thirty to take with us, then by all means, I'm happy staying home while you look for more obsidian."

He'd really thought adventuring would involve less math. "Fine, whatever. Can we light it now?"

She bit her lip. "I guess we can test it to see if it works. Just to see that much, promise?"

He nodded and went running for the flint and steel. When he returned, she was still studying the portal's construction.

The real challenge to portal creation, Max realized, was the plan and the supplies. If someone did it for you, then all you had to worry about was the last step: put a fire in the middle of the portal to activate it. (They ignored the note to include a fermented spider eye in the fire. Max had pulled one out of his pocket but Alison had given him such a glare that he'd put it back.)

Alison bent and pulled her golden helmet out of the chest beside the portal and stroked it. "I still can't believe we got enough gold for me to make a helmet," she said as Max smacked the flint against the steel. "I thought working with rarer elements would make crafting harder, but this gold was actually pretty easy to work with."

"Try enchanting," Max said ruefully. "That's harder."

She glanced up at him. "Is the fire broken?"

He sighed, frustrated, and stood up. "Will you give it a try? You're always better with fire than I am." He handed the tools over. She hesitated and then took them, trading him the helmet to hold. She bent before the portal, trying to get a spark to light.

Right now, all he could see was the clearing on the other side of the portal, grass, flowers, and the woods beyond. But soon, if they'd done everything right, he would see a shimmering portal to another world. He grinned in anticipation. "I can't believe we're finally doing this."

"Neither can I, honestly. I keep expecting something to go wrong," Alison said, striking the flint again. She stood up and took a step back. "I'm still not sure this is the best idea."

"What?" he said, tearing his eyes away from the beautiful black blocks and staring at her. "You're getting too scared to just *activate* it now?"

He pulled the flint and steel from her hands. "Here, I'll do it. Let's just see if it works. Then we can go home. Promise."

Alison was silent. She stared at the portal like it menaced her.

"Aren't you just a little bit curious to see if it works?" he asked desperately.

She gave up and turned away, throwing her hands into the air in frustration. "Fine, activate it, and then we'll go through it because you'll come up with another reason to make me take the next step, and then we'll be transported to another world where we have no idea how to handle ourselves, and then we'll probably die or something worse."

"Yeah, Mom will find out. That would be worse," Max said,

and smacked the flint at the steel a bit harder than he meant to. A spark flared, and then died. "Why do you always anticipate the worst? Sure, we've made mistakes, but look at the things that have gone right!" *Smack*. "We've taught ourselves to craft, enchant, brew potions, even cook. For everything that's gone wrong, we've achieved or learned two things!" *Smack*.

"It doesn't matter how much we've learned! If one thing goes wrong and we're done for, it wouldn't matter if we had the whole knowledge of the Overworld at our fingertips," she said, eyes on the flint and steel. "You're doing that wrong anyway, let me—"

Smack.

Max lost it. "I don't want you to do it! And you know what? I didn't want you to move in! I didn't want my mother to treat you like the daughter she never had and build you an entire wing of the house just for yourself. I didn't want to get grounded and have you take over half of my room!" He struck the steel again. "And you snore."

She whirled on him. "That's a lie," she snarled. She snatched the flint and steel from his hands. "Oh, give me that!"

Smack!

A spark flared.

Alison's eyes went wide, her face bathed in a purple glow.

The air behind Max began to hum and crackle, and he could feel it pulling at him. But he wasn't paying attention to the portal, because he had something else he had to stare at. While they'd been building and then arguing, they had lost track of time. Now the sun hung low in the sky, and the mobs that preferred the dark had come out to see what the fuss was about. From around the cabin, a terrifying green face had peeked, hissing slightly. It emerged, its lengthy, armless body wandering on three legs.

His mind went completely blank. He had been taught the basics of how to avoid a creeper attack—it was something parents taught all children from birth—but the steps completely left his mind. He'd been so excited, and then so angry, and now so shocked. Was he supposed to stay still? Run? Dig a hole and hide in it?

And what would Alison do if she saw it?

The portal's purple glow shed an unworldly light on the clearing. Alison still stared at it, smiling in wonder. She hadn't seen or heard the appearance of the same kind of monster that had destroyed her home. The creeper moved forward on its tripod legs, hissing louder.

Max reached out and took Alison's hand.

"You're right," she said. "This is amazing."

"Alison," he said softly. "We need to run."

"We just got it lit!" she said. "And you haven't even looked at it—" She turned to see what he was staring at, and sucked in her breath in panic.

The creeper was getting closer. It was hissing louder. Alison made a high-pitched, panicked noise deep in her throat. The steel fell to the ground.

"Alison, I can't remember, what do we do?" Max asked, looking around for something to throw at the advancing monster. The creeper began to quiver, and Max could only think of one option left to them. He jumped into the portal, pulling Alison after him. Everything went purple, and dimly he could hear the explosion that indicated the creeper had detonated.

CHAPTER 8

DOOM, SURELY

Disorientation slammed into Alison as the paralyzing fear broke. An odd little part of her mind, watching her impassively, thought it was interesting that her next emotion was not panic. But the world went purple, and then exploded, and then they were on their knees in a very different place.

She was vaguely aware of a popping sound behind them, but the sights and sounds in front were so alien that she could only stare.

They were on their knees in a small mushroom patch, the fungi warm to Alison's fingers. Beyond the patch were vast fields of redstone and bedrock, forming small caverns and stretching up and over them, as if they had fallen into a vast hollow with no exit. Ahead of them was a massive cliff, down which poured a waterfall of lava (*Would that be a lavafall?* a small part of her brain wondered) that pooled at the base and formed a lake. It was beautiful in its terrifying power.

Gouts of flame spawned on various blocks around the lake, burned fiercely, and then died out.

The heat was close to oppressive, but they could breathe at least. Alison took a deep breath and got shakily to her feet.

She squinted, shielding her eyes from the harsh glow off the lava. They stood on rough, brutal, redstone blocks. What was that called? She remembered hearing something about it when people would whisper about the Nether. *Netherrack?*

Around the lake of lava at the base of the cliff flew a few mobs that she had never seen before. Big gray beasts with lazy faces and dangling tentacles wandered the lakeshore making high-pitched, inquisitive noises.

It was amazing. "Max, you were right. I can't believe it, but you were right."

Max was still on his knees, staring behind them. "It's out," he said, his voice high and blank.

"What is?" she asked.

"The portal. The creeper detonated and put it out."

Alison whirled and saw an obsidian rectangle, a doorway that led only to more fire and lava. The glowing purple center was gone, erasing the path back home. Her jaw dropped open.

Max leaped to his feet and ran around the portal, looking at it from all sides. "Alison, relight it! That's all we need to do!"

His volume was increasing as he spoke, and she looked around nervously. She thought she saw one of the floating beasts turn their way, but it could have been a trick of the very low light. Illumination in this cavernous realm came from glowstone nestled in among the bedrock, lava, and not much else. She wished they'd brought torches.

Or the armor and weapons and food and tools they'd left back home, for that matter.

"Max, be quiet, we don't know what's out here," she said, looking nervously at the lava lake. She glanced at her empty hands. "And—and I think I dropped the steel back at the—other portal." She pointed at the flint, lying on the ground where she had dropped it after coming through.

"What? Alison, we can't go home until you relight it!" he shouted. "We aren't prepared, we can't be here!"

She lost all composure then. "*I know that.* Listen," she hissed. "We have to look at our situation, look at our options, and figure something out. We'll be fine. We're surrounded by fire! This won't be hard, but first thing you have to do is be quiet because you're gathering attention we don't need!"

He jerked to a stop as if she'd slapped him, and glared at her. She pointed wordlessly to the lava lake and his eyes widened. "Oh no," he said.

"Oh yeah," she whispered. "So, let's just calm down and see what our options are. We will need to get something to catch on fire and just use that. It'll be fine."

He waved his hands, getting agitated again. "We don't have any fuel!"

They looked around. The area was vast, but she had the sneaking suspicion that any fuel they might find would have already burned to a crisp.

"Well, if we can't go back, we go forward. That Enchanter person, you said they're here, right? Maybe they can help us get home," she said.

"But *we* were supposed to rescue *him*," Max said. "What are we going to say? 'Hi there, we're here to rescue you, if you can tell us how to get home.' That's like the worst rescue attempt ever." In frustration, he grabbed the useless flint from the ground and threw it as far as he could.

He thought he heard a startled sound when it landed, but he dismissed it to face Alison's anger.

"Then what do you think we should do?" she asked, hands on her hips. He said nothing, looking at his feet. "All right, then. Watch those . . . things . . . and if you see them move toward us, let me know. I'm going to see if I can tell where we are."

She ignored his snarky comment that they were in the Nether as she walked away. Just ahead, a rocky spire made of glowstone jutted up from the ground, and Alison approached it cautiously. The heat was almost too much to take, but she could grab the stone and pull herself up. Standing about ten blocks above the ground, she got a much better look at the surrounding area.

Lava was everywhere. Well, not everywhere. There were plenty of places to walk, many directions to go and get lost in. They would have to leave a marker leading back to this place so they didn't lose their way.

A glowing section of rock and lava caught her eye at that moment. It looked as if someone had carved a rough circle into the rock, complete with two dots in the middle. Lava had bubbled up and created a burning image.

Like the cover of the journal.

"Max!" she cried, forgetting her earlier warnings. "He is here! He carved his symbol into the rock! It's a beacon! We can find him and ask him for help!"

She clambered off the rock and ran toward him, only realizing at the last minute that Max was frantically gesturing for her to be quieter.

"Shhhh!" he said. "I thought I heard something."

"Oh, that's those things around the lava, they haven't noticed us," she said, glancing toward the lake.

"No, I thought I heard . . . clucking."

. . .

The beacon didn't matter anymore. The Enchanter, the dormant portal, the lack of weapons and armor, and the very fact that they were surrounded by fire but couldn't actually use any of it to light the portal, nothing mattered. What mattered, the only thing in the world that mattered, was that Max and Alison ran like rabbits trying to escape with their lives while being pursued by wolves.

Only they weren't rabbits, and they weren't being chased by wolves. Instead, behind them ran dozens and dozens of chickens urged on by tiny zombie pigmen atop their backs.

They ran, but Max didn't know or care where. He had outrun zombies before, even the tiny ones. It was a typical way of life in the Overworld when one didn't live in the safety of the villages.

But he had never seen them as zombified pigmen riding chickens. And he had never seen chickens this fast.

Alison wasn't making it any easier. She yelled at Max as they ran, venting her frustrations straight onto his shoulders. "Why did you have to throw the flint at it? Of everything we could have encountered here, we found the fastest, creepiest one, and threw stuff at it! We built the portal because you wanted to build it, and now we're going to be eaten by chickens. I will *not* be eaten by chickens, Max!"

The clucking got louder, and now they could hear the groans and squeaks of the zombie pigmen.

He felt like they had been running forever, zigging and zagging, making abrupt turns when they saw more mobs ahead, but never heading back the way they came, as the chicken jockeys got closer and closer.

Max spied an opening in a cliff, a dark entry into—a cave? Canyon? More death? They didn't have many options.

"Would you stop yelling at me and run?" he said, turning in to the valley while jumping to avoid a geyser of fire erupting to his left. He collided with Alison and she grunted, then tumbled to the ground.

He bent and grabbed her wrist. "Get up!" he shouted, refusing to look at the approaching mob.

"I hope I'm reborn as a sheep so I won't have to worry about meeting you in the next life," she mumbled, but accepted his help getting up and kept running.

"I could be a sheep too, you know," he said. "You don't know. You might be a spider."

"That would be my luck," she said, laughing a little. Her steps slowed a bit as she looked around. "Where are we going?"

The valley stretched out in front of them, cliffs on both sides, and ahead it bent toward the right.

"I wish we could get on top of those cliffs, but they don't look climbable," Max said. "We keep running . . . there." He pointed to where the valley curved, and put on a burst of speed.

When they rounded the corner, they saw that the valley stopped in a dead end, sheer cliffs on three sides, and the only way out was blocked by the approaching mob.

Clucks and grunts echoed off the cliffs, bouncing back and forth, creating a disorienting madhouse of sound.

Running in this direction was not the first bad decision Max had made today, but it was definitely the worst.

So far.

CHAPTER 9

TO A WOLF, IT'S ALL JUST A GAME

A dead end. Max had led them to a dead end. The cliffs ahead of them were sheer except for a small hilly area at the far end of the valley. They might be able to scramble to slightly higher ground. She wasn't sure how high chickens could jump. It was worth a try, at least.

Gouts of fire burst from the netherrack around them, forcing them to dodge or slow down as they rushed for the hill. As they neared it, despair started to replace the panic clutching her chest. The hill wouldn't save them. Nothing but sheer bedrock and netherrack surrounded them. Still they scrambled to get atop the hill and stood, panting, looking around for any escape option.

The chicken jockeys came around the corner, and there were even more than Alison had expected. Not every chicken had a childlike zombie pigman atop its back; others carried full-sized zombie pigmen, their twisted, odd faces focused on Max and Alison. The chicken mounts all moved at about twice the speed of the pint-sized mobs Max and Alison had seen in the Overworld, letting them easily gain on Max and Alison. Twenty chickens and their riders rounded the corner, and then twenty more, and then more, until Alison lost count.

"There's nowhere to go," she whispered.

"We're going to d—" Alison started to say, but stopped when an arrow sailed into the group advancing on them, and pierced both a zombie pigman and his chicken. The monsters fell to the ground, leaving nothing but an egg and a few feathers behind.

"Who's shooting at us? Are we now dealing with skeletons? What's happening?" Max asked, looking for the source of the arrow.

Alison, too, expected to see the jerky white bones firing arrows at them, but now another jockey went down, falling off its chicken and thrashing around on the ground before it popped out of existence.

More went down, and a war cry sounded above their heads. A body fell in front of them and landed in a crouch. Max and Alison both jumped back, and a girl about their own age stood up and turned to them. She grinned and said, "Here, take these."

Then Alison's hands were full of two bows and two quivers. The girl stepped to the side to give herself some room, and then shot another jockey off its chicken.

The girl wore leather armor and had a bow that glowed slightly in the low light. Her hair and skin were light brown. She was followed by a white wolf with a purple kerchief around its neck. The wolf leaped into the group of monsters, snatched a small zombie pigman from a chicken's back, and whipped its head back and forth, the creature in its jaws flailing ineffectually. The wolf tossed it aside and went for another one.

The girl let fly arrow after arrow into the crowd, hitting their attackers with amazing accuracy, spearing others, kicking some zombie pigmen away when they got too close, then shooting them once there was enough space to draw her bow.

The wolf tore through the mob, barking excitedly as if it had never had so much fun. Alison had just thought she was going to die, and the wolf was treating the situation as a game.

"Ali, shoot them!" Max said, grabbing a bow and quiver from her. "She can't get them all!"

Alison wasn't so sure this girl couldn't take down the entire horde herself, but the mobs were converging on her, and she couldn't kill them fast enough to keep free of them. One reached out and grabbed the girl's arm, slashing at her, and she leaped aside, off-balance for a moment.

Alison slid down the hill, aimed, and took a deep breath. Now she was ready.

The bow wasn't well made. She guessed it had been dropped by a monster. Still, better than nothing. It would shoot an arrow, and that's all she needed. She quickly drew and let fly an arrow at a chicken and its rider that had pushed the girl to the ground and were threatening to overwhelm her. The zombie pigman fell, and Alison took another one down. The wolf came to the rescue then, barreling through and knocking jockeys and chickens aside to reach its mistress. The girl got to her feet with a grateful nod toward Alison, and nocked another arrow.

Alison took a quick survey of the scene. She didn't want to hit the girl or the wolf, so she went for some of the straggling beasts bringing up the rear. Her first shot went wide, but her second struck home. Where was Max? She hadn't seen any of his arrows going into the monsters, but she didn't dare turn around and look for her friend.

Another guttural cry, and Max appeared in the middle of the melee, swinging a golden sword. (*A golden sword? Where did he get that?*) He wasn't very good; he hadn't had a lot of practice, and Alison had refused all his requests to spar with the swords she created. But sometimes all you needed was a sharp weapon and an enemy in front of you, and then gravity and inertia did the rest.

After that, the tide turned. Max and the wolf took care of the mobs from the middle of the fight while Alison and the other girl attacked from the fringes.

In a few short minutes, it was over. They were surrounded by dropped weapons, arrows, eggs, rotten flesh, and gold nuggets. Alison and Max panted and leaned on each other, but the girl looked positively triumphant.

"Did we win?" Max asked, looking around at the loot, Alison, and the strange girl who had saved them.

"I think so," Alison said, nodding. The other girl looked satisfied watching her wolf run around, gobbling up rotten flesh. "Hey, thanks for saving us. Where did you come from, anyway?"

The girl pushed her long brown hair out of her face and inspected a bright red burn on her arm. Then she put her hands on her hips and looked at Alison. "What were *you* doing running straight into an ambush? They herded you here! Didn't you realize that?" She grinned at Alison, taking some of the sting from her words.

"We got lost," Alison said. "And then we were running for our lives. We didn't really think."

The girl looked them over, appraising. "That's how you die real fast around here. Another way to die here is to visit looking like that." She pointed at their clothes. "Where's your portal? We'll get you back safely. You won't survive half a day here without weapons and armor."

"It's that way," Alison said, pointing to the left.

"No it isn't, it's definitely that way," Max said, pointing to the right.

"It was right near that spire of glowstone," Alison said. "Back that way."

"Which spire of glowstone? Those things are all over," the girl said.

"We—ran a long way. I'm not sure where we started. We'll have to go look for it. It's not like it's going anywhere."

"A creeper blew up and put out the portal as we came through. We weren't prepared to relight it."

"We weren't prepared for anything," Alison said.

Max stuck his hand out. "I'm Max. She's Alison."

"Freya," the girl said, shaking it. She shook Alison's hand too. "And that's a mess. Come on, I live just up here." She pointed to the top of the cliff.

Max had too many questions to know which one to ask first. How had three kids and a wolf demolished a huge mob of chicken jockeys? Who was the amazing girl who had rescued them? How did she get that burn on her arm? Who had built the secret tunnel in the canyon wall that led up to her fortress—and how did she have a fortress?!

But honestly, the biggest thing on his mind was the glorious sword at his belt.

One of the zombie pigmen had dropped it after Freya had shot it with an arrow. It fell, twitching, and before it disappeared from the world, it dropped the sword with a clang.

His basic understanding of enchantment told him there was something special about the sword that went beyond the golden beauty of its crafting. He'd have to give it to Alison for her to check out and make sure it wasn't damaged or about to break or anything, but he wanted to answer the biggest question: *What was it enchanted with?*

His hand kept going to the hilt resting against his hip, and then he would let it go. It wasn't time to think about this. He had to figure out what was going on and, more importantly, how to get home. Once they found what they were looking for, of course.

Alison had the job of "ask the girl all the questions" well in control. Freya led them up the tunnel, casually packing away the loot she had gathered. Alison followed her closely, gathering information even as she looked with amazement at the tunnel around them, glistening with redstone and the occasional glow-stone.

"So, you live here?" she asked. "How is that possible? I thought all the buildings here were infested with"—she waved her hand vaguely behind them—"those mobs."

"Oh, blazes infested the place when I moved in. They still do," Freya said. "Skeletons too, sometimes. That's why I built the tunnel. There's usually nothing in the canyon. The mobs are stupid and don't think that a building can have a back door. I cleared out most of the mobs when I took the place over, but there are always more outside. I had to go out the front door to get to you, though, since the tunnel takes more time." She indicated her burned arm. "That's how I got this."

She turned and winked at Alison. "But the best part is, the mobs outside also guard it from anything or anyone else trying to get inside. They don't realize that they actually serve as my guardians. Although the kind of guardian that will kill you, too, if they get a chance, so they're not perfect." She turned and continued walking. The tunnel was now spiraling upward at a sharper angle.

"So, there aren't any of those things inside?" Alison asked.

"Who knows?" Freya shrugged as if Alison was asking about vermin, not deadly creatures. "It's a big fortress, after all. They could spawn anywhere. I keep the rooms lit, and my wolf patrols as best she can. I mainly live in just a few rooms, and keep the rest closed off unless I need something. There's mad loot in these fortresses, and I haven't explored all of this one."

"Why not?" Max asked, forgetting about his sword once he had the hint that there might be more elsewhere.

"I have everything I need," Freya said. "I've got mushrooms for food, mob hunting for entertainment, and this mutt for companionship." She looked back at them and smiled, but her eyes looked sunken and dark, as if she hadn't slept well in months.

Alison frowned at Freya. Max recognized that look; she gave it to him all the time. It was the *I know you're not telling me everything* look.

"Where's your family?" Alison asked when they reached a door.

Freya didn't turn around, but she stopped briefly. "We'll have to see if I have enough potions to fix our wounds," she said, as if Alison hadn't spoken. "And we can take inventory and get something to eat. That mob dropped a lot of choice loot."

Freya swung open the door, and Alison's stomach gurgled when she saw it was a well-stocked storeroom. "Come on in."

CHAPTER 10

TO THE VICTOR GOES THE SPOILED MEAT

Alison was famished. Max had cooked for them, proudly showing off his new skills with the furnace, and she had never eaten anything as good as the chicken that dropped from the mobs. She tried not to think that she had recently looked this chicken in the eye— but then again, that chicken and its jockey had tried to kill her, so she had every right to defend herself and eat the spoils of war.

Freya had cooked some rotten meat for her wolf, over by the window so that the smell wouldn't permeate the room. She tossed several charred green pieces to the happy pet as she told her story.

"This is Bunny Biter. I've had her since she was a pup. She was deathly afraid of rabbits." Freya laughed. "She'll bite the head off a baby zombie, but show her a long-eared hopping thing and she runs away. I named her Bunny Biter hoping it would give her some confidence, but it didn't help. Then we found out that there aren't any rabbits here anyway. But the name stuck." She tossed the last bit of meat to Bunny Biter and wiped her hands on her pants. "So, are you two brother and sister?"

Max and Alison shared a glance, and then Alison said, "No, not exactly. I moved in with Max's family when mine—well, I'm on my own now." Her throat suddenly felt swollen, and no more words would force themselves out.

Freya frowned and sat down next to Alison at the table. "What do you mean?" she asked.

Alison didn't answer. Max looked at her, and then back at Freya. "Creeper attack. Blew up her whole house. Wiped out her family. She's the only survivor."

"The only survivor," Freya said quietly. She took a breath, and it caught in her throat. "I'm—I'm really sorry."

She got up and turned her back to them, breathing deeply.

Alison cleared her throat and took a deep breath. "Max's family took me in. They live nearby. Nearby my old house, I mean, not nearby here. Nothing is nearby here." Freya still didn't turn around. Alison looked at Max, who shrugged. "But you knew that. Right. Our families were friends, and they let me live with them," she finished, wishing she hadn't gone on that tangent.

"Are you okay?" Max asked, looking at Freya.

She didn't turn around.

"Um, Freya?" he said.

"Yeah?" she said brightly, and turned around. Her cheeks were red and her eyes were wide. Alison studied her, tilting her head.

"Are you okay?" he repeated.

"Oh, I thought you were talking to Alison." She frowned. "Are *you* okay?"

"Uh, yeah, I think I will be, anyway," Alison said. "Thanks."

"That was good of you," Freya said to Max. She was talking faster than normal. "It's good to have friends." She had a faraway, sad look in her eyes.

"What about you? How did you end up alone here?" Alison asked.

Freya blinked, and snapped back to the present. "Right. Well, my family were travelers, they liked wandering around and exploring. We'd arrive in an area, build a basic house there, learn about the area, visit the villages, whatever, and then move on." She chuckled. "My mom always said we were planting cabins like other people plant trees."

Alison wondered if Freya was attached somehow to the Enchanter, but if she was, Max would have been far more interested in her. Now he stared out the window at the patrolling mobs far below the cliff.

"Anyway, my dad said we had explored all the biomes in the Overworld and got it in his head that we needed to explore the Nether. He got obsidian from this dealer who lives near a lava flow, and got plans for a portal—he spent our entire savings to do so—and we came here."

"Where's your portal?" Max asked eagerly.

Freya shrugged. "I don't know. It's probably still around somewhere. But we got here a while ago. Mom mapped out our path so we could get back, but then we found a bunch of blazes. Or they found us. Same thing that happened to you." She chewed on her lip for a moment. "I . . . made it out alive. The map was on Mom when she"—Freya cleared her throat, and then continued—"and I had to run. I had Bunny Biter, and my bow, and my armor. And that apple," she added, pointing to an apple sitting atop a stone table in the corner that Alison hadn't noticed yet.

"I'm so sorry," Alison said. "I know how you feel."

Freya kept staring at the apple, a friendly bright red that stood out against all the dark red-gray around them. "So . . . you haven't eaten it yet?" Max asked, frowning.

Alison stared at him. "That's what you think is important? Really?"

He shrugged. "If it's the only fruit around here, then yeah, maybe."

"It reminds me of them," Freya said defensively.

Alison had a necklace of her mother's and some old letters of her father's. She hadn't thought of saving food. But she hadn't had to.

"I'd think you'd want to eat any food you can in a place like this," Max continued.

"And I'd think you wouldn't come through a portal without being fully prepared to deal with the Nether, but we all make weird decisions in our lives," Freya snapped.

"What do you do for water?" Alison asked, trying to defuse the growing tension. "It doesn't spawn here naturally, right?"

Freya laughed and wiped at her cheeks. "Oh yeah, there's no water here. I was in charge of carrying all our water. When I took over this place, I found a few cauldrons of water and made some more. I store them in a side room." She pointed to a door on the wall opposite the secret tunnel. "If I meet another traveler, I figure I could try to barter with them for more water. It's worked before."

"Why haven't you gone home?" Max said quietly. "You said your portal is still out there. Aren't you even *trying* to find it?"

Freya looked down at Bunny Biter, who looked up hopefully to see if she had found any more zombie pigman bits to feed her. "This is home now," she said. "I have Bunny Biter, I have a house, I have a mushroom farm."

"But that doesn't make any sense," Max said. "This is the *Nether*. No one lives here!"

"I have nothing!" Freya cried. "My family was all I had. No

one's waiting for me in the Overworld. I know how to survive here. Why not stay?"

Alison stared at her, finally coming around to Max's point of view. She pointed out the window and looked at Freya. "Why *not* stay here? There are about a million reasons! Your water is going to run out! There's a lake of fire! Mobs of chickens and zombie pigmen! The fact that you can't enter rooms in your own house because, oh, well, there may be deadly mobs on the other side of the door! And eating nothing but mushrooms and whatever you can hunt off a deadly monster for the rest of your life? Are you insane?" She looked back out into the canyon where one jockeyless chicken still wandered around, pecking sadly at a patch of soul sand.

Max came away from the window, rubbing his ear like he did when he was thinking. "Ali's not wrong," he said to Freya. "No one in their right mind would want to live here." He looked back at Alison, with uncharacteristic maturity in his eyes. "But Ali," he said, his voice soft. "Were you in *your* right mind when your parents died?"

Alison's jaw snapped shut as she thought about that terrible day. The tree house, obliterated. The sheep, escaped. Her parents, sister, grandmother, nowhere to be found. Common sense had been to find a neighbor, get help searching what was left of the house, looking in the area for injured family members.

Instead, she had numbly gone after the sheep. Soon after, Max's frantic mother and Mr. Hatch found her. They had heard the explosion and were doing the right thing in the situation: searching for survivors. Alison had just wandered off, being useless.

"I have to get the sheep into the pen," she'd said. Her eyes had felt very wide, and she'd stared at the adults, not focusing on them.

Max's mom had looked at Mr. Hatch for one anguished minute, and then carefully wrapped Alison in a hug. That's when she'd allowed herself to cry.

Alison shook her head to clear it of the memory, wanting to physically push it away. She glanced at Freya, who was petting her wolf and pointedly ignoring Max and Alison. "No. I'm sorry," Alison said. "We can leave in the morning."

Freya looked up at them, confusion scrawled across her face. "Leave? Why would you leave? You'll die out there!" She shook her head firmly. "No, you're staying here with me. I'm going to show you the fortress—the *safe* rooms," she added at the look on Alison's face, "because I think you're really going to want to see the special room."

"The 'special room'?" Max asked, his hand closing around the hilt of his new sword. Alison wasn't even sure if he knew he was doing it.

Freya nodded confidently. "Oh yeah. That's where the fun stuff is."

CHAPTER 11

THE LOCKED ROOM IS MIGHTIER
THAN THE SWORD

Freya had initially taken them to what Max and Alison had as-
sumed was a kitchen in the fortress, as it held the secret door to
the tunnel outside, as well as a furnace for cooking and a few tables. But Max realized quickly that whoever, or whatever, had
constructed the fortress meant it as merely a storage room. That
much was obvious when Freya led them out of the room and the
glory of the great hall lay before them.

"I don't like to eat in here," she admitted.

"Oh, really? Why not?" Max asked, sarcastically, his voice
sounding tiny in the massive room.

The ceiling created a cavern at least thirty blocks high, with a
large carved blaze on the far wall. Around the blaze a cascade of
lava ran down the wall to flow into some other area—hopefully
not another place in the fortress, because this room was hot
enough. Down the middle of the room ran a stone table that
could seat at least fifty people, possibly more. The stone chairs
were the only source of color in the room; about ten of them had

colorful cushions on the seats, making those chairs stand out garishly.

Freya saw Ali touching one of the cushions. "Yeah, I added my own touches to begin with. Found a stash of wool banners and repurposed them to make the cushions."

"You found a stash of banners in the Nether?" Ali asked, frowning.

"I figured someone from the Overworld brought them," Freya said, shrugging. "Who knows where stuff comes from?"

Max had hoped that the great hall would be the only lava room. No such luck. When they exited the hall and entered an even bigger cavern, he jumped back at the steep drop into a river of lava below them.

"I call this the Hub," Freya said, striding confidently onto a stone ledge only two blocks wide. It was the first step of a bridge that led from the hall in several directions, with a doorway at the end of each branch going into the sheer rock wall at the other end of the cavern.

Oh yeah, and the bridges were keeping them high—at least fifty blocks high—above a river of lava below. *Guess that's where the lava from the great hall went.*

"So where do all those doors go?" Ali asked.

Freya pointed to the leftmost door. "That one goes to the living quarters. Bunny Biter and I sleep on a blanket on the floor in one of those rooms. Do you want to know the real proof that the Nether is pure evil?" She stepped out onto the bridge over the lava and kept talking as if she expected them to follow. With nervous glances down into the glowing orange fire death below, they complied. "If you try to sleep in a bed you'll blow up as if you tried to snuggle with a creeper." Freya gave a quick glance over her shoulder at Ali, who was pale. "Oh, crap, I'm sorry. But yeah. You'll blow up."

"If we sleep in a bed?" Ali asked, her words slow, as if she was making sure she understood the meaning of each one.

"Yeah. I don't know what it is about this place. Can't sleep in a bed. Dad always said it was insta-death." Freya shrugged, not looking back at them. "He could have been lying but I really didn't feel like testing it. Kind of like testing if a sword is sharp by trying to cut your arm off."

"Tell me again how I was not in my right mind when my parents died," Ali hissed at Max. "Where are we going to sleep, on top of a lava raft?"

Max grinned at her. "It would be warm, at least."

"Second door," continued Freya, "is the kitchen, and beyond that, the main living area. It's got a gorgeous balcony that looks out over the canyon."

"And that's where you make gallons of mushroom soup?" Ali asked.

"That's right," Freya said. "Third door is the one we're going to. That's the basement where the library is. Enchanting, alchemy, crafting, it's all done down there. Wait till you see it."

They reached the crossroads where the bridge branched, and Freya took the third path. Max looked down again at the roiling lava below them and then hurried to keep up. Sweat beaded on his brow from the rising heat.

"What about that?" he asked, pointing to where the last bridge on the right ended at two stacked blocks of netherrack.

"I'm pretty sure the spawn rooms are beyond there. We don't go there," Freya said. "There are some bedrooms I don't open, but I've made sure to clear out the basement and we try to clean it every day. The stuff down there is too useful to keep locked up."

They walked down a few flights of stairs. Max ran his hand along the stone wall, feeling the heat come and go as they went below the level of the lava lake.

They reached a metal door at the bottom of the stairs. Freya held up a hand and gestured for them to be quiet. She placed a hand on the door for a moment and then took it off.

"Hot?" Max whispered. Freya shook her head and put her hand to her lips, glaring at him.

He got the message and stopped talking. She put her head to the door and listened, then frowned. She looked back at them and walked stiffly around, miming shooting an arrow. Ali nodded, getting it, and Max realized Freya was telling them there were skeletons inside.

Freya pointed to Ali and then partway up the stairs, giving a little distance between her and the door. She pointed to Max and then at the door. She went to join Ali, who had already removed her bow.

Wait, why did *he* have to be point? That wasn't fair. Freya was a better fighter than he was!

But the weapons. He had a new, possibly enchanted golden sword, and everyone knows the sword fighter has to get into the fight while the ranged fighters pick off the enemy from a distance.

Why hadn't he picked up a bow? He drew his sword and moved directly in front of the door. The golden sword thrummed in his hand, and he knew he had chosen the right thing. He wouldn't have traded the sword for anything.

Now he could hear it, the faint clacking sound that the skeletons always made when they were hunting for prey.

He put his left hand on the knob and gripped the sword tighter with his right. He gave a quick glance back and saw that the girls behind him both had arrows nocked, ready to let fly at a moment's notice.

Max took a deep breath, opened the door, and, with a primal yell, ran into the room.

Bunny Biter streaked past him, tripping him, which saved his life. As he stumbled, a sword *whooshed* over his head as a skeleton by the door swung at him. Bunny Biter grabbed the skeleton's sword arm in her teeth and bit down hard, her weight dragging the skeleton's arm down. She shook her head quickly, and Max took the skeleton's head off with the sword. He didn't pay much attention to the body, instead watching the head fly off into the room. He took a moment to appreciate his new sword, staring at the way the lava light glinted off the gilded metal.

It really needed a name, he decided.

Another skeleton lunged at him just as he heard the twang of an arrow—it was coming from inside the room, and it was headed for him. He fell against the open door, the arrow hitting the metal and ricocheting off. The air *whooshed* in front of him as the skeleton missed its swing, inches from Max's face.

"Max, get out of the doorway!" Ali called from the hallway, exasperated. "We don't have a clear shot!"

"I hear you," he grumbled. "Kinda busy!" He slid off the door and toward the right corner of the room. He got a sense of how massive the room was: it was a long library with bookshelves, enchanting tables, and more. It reminded him of the Enchanter's basement, but bigger and more ornate.

This one was also full of skeletons.

How were they going to get through them all? He didn't have time to worry, though, since one was coming straight at him. But the dang wolf was under his feet again, and he stumbled and fell, his back against the wall and the skeleton above him, raising its sword to attack. He had no idea how he was going to get out of this one, but he tried to block the incoming blow with his own, still nameless weapon. He felt a thrum of power when the swords connected, and the skeleton flew backward into the crowd where it was immediately shot by one of the girls in the hallway.

The skeleton fell, and Bunny Biter ran up to it, grabbed its collarbone, and shook it hard. The skeleton was clearly down, so maybe this was just to make sure, or to get a snack before the thing disappeared. But the wolf dropped its prize and ran for her next target.

Max clambered up, staring at the fallen skeleton. He was beginning to get an idea about the potential power his sword might be carrying. He kept away from the doorway to give the archers their chance to shoot straight into the room. Two more enemies fell immediately to arrows, but then Max was busy again, dodging an arrow from a skeleton across the room. As much as he wanted to attack that one in retaliation, he had another in front of him to deal with. He swung his sword and connected with its ribs. It flew off its feet and backward, crashing into the attacker that had just fired the arrow.

Oh! That was interesting. He focused on another skeleton, again testing his new sword theory. The skeleton was swinging a sword at him. Instead of landing a blow, he parried the strike, and when the weapons connected, the skeleton flew backward.

This was fun! With renewed energy, Max waded into the melee, swinging at anything that moved, not trying to kill, but just to connect. Every time he touched an enemy, it flew backward into the wall or deeper into the room. Bunny Biter was having a party, gleefully barking and chasing the skeletons around as they ran from her, and going from fallen skeleton to fallen skeleton. She was rewarded with more bones as the walking undead fell.

It was becoming almost a game. Bunny Biter kept the skeletons moving; the arrows flying into the room were taking down several; and the distractions allowed him to go on the offensive, bellowing and swinging his new sword to knock back the monsters. *We'll survive the Nether. This is easy!* The thought had barely formed in his adrenaline-filled mind when he heard Ali's cry of alarm. He didn't have time to register what it meant because he was distracted by the sudden piercing pain of an arrow sinking into his shoulder.

Alison knelt over Max, who lay on the floor. "Are you sure you don't have a cot or something to put him on?" she asked.

"Told you what happens when you get in a bed here," Freya said, tossing a torch onto the wall and running for a brewing stand. "Just try to make him comfortable."

With what? Ali thought, but said nothing. She started reciting the rules of mob encounters that they had learned in school.

"*Don't remove the arrow until you have a healing potion,*" she said aloud, and tore Max's shirt from where the arrow had pierced his shoulder.

"*Carefully secure the arrow,*" she said, repeating the words of the next step.

"*Brew a healing potion,*" she said, but Freya had that covered. She was still at the brewing station, red liquid bubbling in her glass beaker as she added ingredients.

"*Keep an eye out for further threats, as you will be vulnerable during this time.*" She glanced around her. Bunny Biter was bounding through the room, gathering fallen skeleton bones and taking them to a corner. She couldn't dig here, but she clearly had a special place for her treats. *I guess it keeps the place tidy.* The wolf wasn't exactly keeping vigilant watch, but she was moving around the room a lot, so if there were any stray threats, Bunny Biter would run into them.

"Tell the injured what an idiot they are," she said, making up this rule on the spot. "You are an idiot," she said. "I told you to stay out of the doorway."

"What do you think of 'Bone Bane'?" Max mumbled.

Alison sat back, staring at him. She was as happy to see him awake as she was confused by his comment. "What are you talking about?"

"My . . . sword." He waved his uninjured arm to gesture at his hip, where his sword would have been. He'd dropped it when he fell, and it lay off to the side. Bunny Biter was sniffing it now. "Needs a name. It's magic."

"That's what you're thinking about?" Alison shouted. "Max, you were *shot*."

"But did you see the sword? It's got . . . a knockback enchantment!" he said, excitement coming through even as he was wincing from pain.

"You're impossible," she said. She stood stiffly and walked to where Freya was swirling the red liquid in a bottle.

"How's the patient?" Freya asked.

"Fine. Talking about his sword." Alison rolled her eyes. "Is it ready?"

"Yes," Freya said, handing the bottle to her. Between them, Bunny Biter walked, backward, as she awkwardly dragged Max's new sword away by the hilt.

Freya held Max's head while Alison poured the potion into his mouth. Max choked at first, coughed, and then drank the rest. He sighed, and lay back. Alison adjusted his head and shoulder so his healing body could push the arrow out easily.

The arrow trembled and jerked, and then rose out of Max's shoulder, falling to the side. He sighed again, and closed his eyes.

"Let him sleep," Freya said, and sat down, leaning against the wall. "I could use some too."

Now that Max was all right, the adrenaline rushed out of Alison, and she began to shake. She tried to smoothly move from kneeling by Max to leaning against the wall by Freya, but it was closer to just falling over. She was glad the wall was there to catch her.

Freya cracked an eyelid. "What's with you? Are you hurt?"

"I'm not used to so much fighting. And—" She closed her mouth with a snap. She didn't want to say it.

"And?"

Alison closed her eyes so she wouldn't have to see Freya. "I was the one that shot Max," she whispered.

She waited for a blurt of horror, or an accusation, or a demand she return her bow, or, well, anything other than Freya saying, "So?" in a bored voice.

But that was what she said. Alison opened her eyes and looked at her new friend, who rested with her head back against the wall. "What do you mean 'So'? I shot my best friend! I'm a monster!"

"We were fighting. You told him to stay out of the doorway. You shot a bow into a melee. He got shot. Friendly fire happens all the time in battles."

"I never really thought about it," Alison said. Fighting clearly had some important details other than "kill the monster, and don't let the monster kill you."

"You shot him, but you also took care of him and made sure he got treatment. Now he's fine." She glanced at Max, shirtless and dozing on his back. "I'll need to find him another shirt, though."

Alison had nearly fallen asleep when Freya started talking. She sat against the wall, her butt nearly numb, her neck stiff from leaning back, but she didn't move when Freya's words jerked her out of her doze. It took her a second to catch up, but Alison quickly realized she was talking about her parents' death.

"To be honest I didn't know what to do, so I did what was in front of me," she said. She had stretched out on the floor on her back, head pillowed on Bunny Biter, who had returned to them with a rib bone in her mouth and was happily chewing away. The slurping and grinding sounds were oddly soothing.

"All I could think to do was solve the problem I had at the moment," Freya continued. "Run from the mobs. Get something to eat. Find a safe place to rest. I didn't have time to look for the portal. Every time I thought about backtracking to find it, something got in my way. Usually a blaze. Sometimes a chicken."

Alison grimaced, the expression having nothing to do with her stiff neck. "You couldn't think about the big picture. When everything's so big that you can't pick out which one's important, you just deal with the little stuff."

"Because you can control the little stuff," Freya said, nodding.

"Yeah," Alison said. "I remember."

"How long has it been?" Freya asked.

Alison thought. She hadn't really been keeping track of time, but the sheep had escaped three times, and they had ruined Max's mom's farm, and Mr. Hatch's ranch, and there had been time for

Max's mom to build and then tear down the tower she'd made for Alison.

"A few months, maybe?" she ventured. "I'm not sure, really."

"It's been about six months for me," Freya said, "although it's really hard to judge time down here. No sun." She glanced up, toward the ceiling. "That's one of the things I miss."

"I figured you'd miss a bed," Alison grumbled.

"Well, Bunny Biter is a good pillow, and a good guard wolf," Freya said. "I don't need much."

Alison wanted to tell her she needed more than a mushroom farm and a wolf pillow, but didn't feel like getting into an argument. "It's weird that we're so different," she said instead.

Freya stroked the wolf's shoulder. "What do you mean?"

"We're dealing with the same awful situation," Alison said. "And you're running through the Nether on an adventure, and I just went to a friend's house in the woods and wondered whether I should fix the sheep pen or let them go." She paused and sighed, not ready to keep talking but knowing she had to get this out. "I've been so afraid, and so sad. And compared to you, I've had nothing to worry about. Freya, you're so strong. You live in the *Nether*."

"Nothing to worry about? You just said Max's family lived out in the woods," Freya said. "Don't you still have to deal with the occasional creeper or skeleton? Certainly spiders."

Alison thought for a second and remembered the lava cave and the skeletons. She remembered the creeper that had blown up and ruined their portal. "Well, yeah, but I didn't really think about that when it was happening. I only thought about what to do next to survive. I didn't worry about my . . . my situation." She still had trouble saying *my dead family and my destroyed home.*

"Sounds familiar," Freya said.

The realization hit Alison then. Freya was afraid of confronting her own problems. That was why she was living in this incredibly dangerous world. Who worried about dead parents when deadly monsters were behind half the doors in your house? She felt conflicted; part of her felt sorry for Freya, that she was unwilling or unable to deal with this emotional trauma, and part of her was kind of jealous that Freya didn't have to deal with it. Still, Alison didn't want to have to live in the Nether to run away from her problems. No problem was that bad.

"I haven't thought about what would have happened if this had happened to me in the Overworld," Freya said. "But we didn't really have a permanent home anyway, so I would probably be doing the same thing, just with better food and more company."

"And a bed," added Alison. "And I don't know how I would have reacted if this had happened to me in the Nether. Situations are unique that way, huh?"

"You don't think you could have handled yourself here, if you'd been equipped?" Freya asked. "I guess you'll never know. And I hope you never have to."

Alison laughed, the bitter sound surprising even herself. "Well, I'm without my family and I'm stuck in the Nether, so I guess I have more in common with you than I thought. We just got here in different ways."

"Guess you're right," Freya said.

"Come back with us," Alison blurted. "When we find our way home. You can have a bed. You can have security. Water. Colors! Oh, I miss green," she added with sudden surprise.

"And," Max said, his voice thick from sleep, "we have almost no lava compared to you." He sat up, blinking, rolling his previously injured shoulder that showed no sign of an arrow wound.

Freya shook her head. "No, I already decided, this is my home now." She sat up and looked at the room that had recently spawned enough skeletons to easily kill them.

"But home isn't a place," Alison said slowly. "It's wherever you are comfortable enough to sleep."

Max made a face at her and looked pointedly at where each of them was trying to get quick, uncomfortable rest.

She frowned and shook her head. "No, I don't mean napping on a stone floor. I mean real sleep, where you don't think anything is going to kill you. Sleep where you're comfortable enough to sleep all night, where you trust the people with you, where you wake up happy and wanting to share breakfast and then go and rebuild the garden you accidentally destroyed with lava yesterday." She missed Max's mom, then, and knew that she must be going mad with worry right now.

"That's weirdly specific," Freya said, closing her eyes again. "But I guess I get your meaning."

"So, you'll come back with us?" Alison asked hopefully.

"No," Freya said, settling back into Bunny Biter's soft belly. "And if you want to see exactly why I won't, go and look around this room and ask yourself if you could leave it. Now be quiet. I need sleep."

"Freya," Alison said quietly. Freya cracked her left eye open again and regarded her. "I don't think we can find our portal on our own. You know the mobs and the terrain. We'll die out there without your help. And we want to go home."

Freya sighed and sat up, resigned to the fact that she wasn't going to get any sleep. "I'll help you find your portal, or another one," she said. "After that, I can't promise anything. But we've got to sort through our loot and get you some proper equipment first."

CHAPTER 12

THE ENCHANTER WITH NO NAME

Once cleared of monsters, the basement workshop was really a thing of beauty, making the Enchanter's crafting room look like Max's parents' storage shed.

Now that he was feeling better and there weren't any mobs trying to kill him, Max could take a more leisurely trip around the room. Freya's fortress had four enchanting tables, four brewing stands, five furnaces, and the walls were lined with alternating chests and bookcases, most of the books glowing or glittering with ripe enchantments. Basic crafting workbenches lined another wall.

"Did you build all these?" he asked.

"I carried a few tables with me into the Nether, but most of these were here when I got here," she said, busying herself at a brewing stand.

"Then who built them?" he asked.

She shrugged. "I assume the same person who built the fortress. There are buildings all over the place; some of them have equipment in them, some don't."

"Where do you think the person who built this building went? Why build in the Nether?" he persisted.

"I don't know, Max," she said, putting down her flask and looking at him. "I didn't really think about it while I was looking for a safe place to rest, where things wouldn't kill me."

"I was just asking," he grumbled. "It's a valid question."

At the far end of the room were twelve chests lined up under torches. Eleven were regular torches, but the twelfth was lit with redstone, giving off a dire light.

High on the walls were more carvings, some of blazes, others of skeletons, endermen, or, bizarrely, chickens.

Freya moved along one wall, pointing to each chest and bookcase. "That has food, more than mushroom soup. I try to ration it, so don't gorge yourselves. That one has all different kinds of metal, that one has gemstones, and that one has different woods. The last chest has all the crap that won't fit in the first several.

"The books aren't as organized. I can't find any reason why they're on any specific shelf; I only know that they don't want to be shelved anywhere but where they are. Try to move them and they just pop back out. And those"—she pointed to the torchlit chests on the far side of the room—"are for finished items."

"What's in the red one?" Max asked immediately. His hands itched to open the chests, but he knew better than to go rummaging through them. He'd tried it once, and had definitely learned his lesson.

"I haven't been through that one yet," Freya admitted. "I figured the red torch was a warning." She grinned at him. "But you're welcome to try."

Max started forward but Alison caught his arm, dropping the helmet she had been inspecting. "Are you kidding me?" she hissed in his ear. "Of all the chests in the room, you have to go for the most dangerous?"

"You don't know it's the most dangerous," he said, jerking his arm away.

"So why are you in the Nether anyway?" Freya asked, going to a chest by a brewing stand and searching through it.

"Max wants to rescue someone," Alison said, heading for the chest that Freya had said held metals, clutching the helmet under her arm. "I just want to get home."

"We can get home after we find the Enchanter," Max said, looking at the twelve chests greedily. "The portal won't be going anywhere." He wondered what each chest held, but paused. What if the last chest was dangerous after all? He reached out for the latch on the red-lit chest, but froze when Freya and Alison spoke at the same time:

"Have you come across anyone else since you got here?" Freya asked, as Alison said, outrage rising in her voice, "What do you mean, 'The portal won't be going anywhere'? Are you saying we aren't looking for the portal?"

"No, have you?" Max asked Freya, ignoring Alison.

She shook her head. "Not really. I haven't seen anyone except you, my family, and that one old guy."

"Max—what's more important than us finding the portal home? You don't even know this Enchanter person!" Alison shouted.

Max motioned for Freya to keep talking. "*What* old guy?"

"He was in the same canyon as you two," Freya said, adding something to the brewing stand. "He was carving a symbol in the canyon wall when blazes attacked him. I got him out of there and tried to give him a place to stay and some food, but he turned me down, saying he didn't deserve it, or something." She frowned. "He was weird. Kind of sad. I asked what kind of person didn't deserve help in the Nether and he didn't answer. He accepted food and stayed here for a night to take care of his injuries, but then just ran away. I figured he must be a madman, or some kind of criminal."

"Am I talking to myself?" Alison asked. "Hello?"

"What did the symbol look like?" Max demanded. "The one that he was carving? Did you erase it?"

Freya looked at him with irritation. "No, I didn't erase it. But a lava spring did cover it. It was—"

Max interrupted her, pulling the journal out of his pack. "Did it look like this?" he asked, holding it up to her: the Enchanter's symbol burned into the cover.

Freya glanced up and then back at her brewing stand. "Yeah, that was it. He was really upset about some—"

Max dropped the book with a resounding thud. Bunny Biter looked up from where she had been gnawing on a skeleton leg bone and made a small whine deep in her throat. "When was this? Where did he go?" he demanded.

"A few weeks ago, I guess," Freya said, looking up and frowning at him. "It's hard to judge time here, you know. And I have no idea where he went."

Alison stared at him. "What is wrong with you? Are you okay?"

"No, I'm not okay. Nothing is okay," he said, running his hands through his hair in agitation. He'd been *so close.* And he hadn't even thought to ask if the Enchanter had been there the moment they'd met Freya. They'd let themselves get distracted, and now there was no clue where he was.

Max scrubbed his face with his hands. He stood abruptly and left the room, heading back up to the Hub.

Only when he reached the top of the stairs did he realize that he had no idea where his sword, Bone Bane, was.

"What was all that about?" Freya asked, turning to Alison, whose head had disappeared back into the metals chest.

"He's been single-minded in his quest to find this Enchanter person ever since he found that journal. I don't know why, really, since the journal is terrible. The guy was a really bad enchanter and alchemist. Now Max wants to find him more than he wants to get home. I don't get it."

"It sounds like he's taking this personally," Freya said. "Did he know this Enchanter guy or something?"

"No, he's never even said if he knows the name . . ." Alison looked up, covering her mouth with her hand. "Oh. *Oh*." She chewed on her lip a moment. "Did the old guy who came here give you his name?"

"Nicholas," Freya said.

Alison turned and went running after Max.

CHAPTER 13

LIES AND SOUP

"*Is that* architect *coming over tonight?*" *The cross voice came out of the attic. Grandma Dia was spinning wool in her small bedroom, which she liked to do in the afternoon when the light was "just right."*

"*All the architects are coming over, Grandma,*" *Alison said. She liked teasing her grandma, knowing exactly whom she was talking about. Max's eccentric Uncle Nicholas and her grandparents knew each other from long ago, but didn't seem to have been friends. Their time together had apparently been filled with a lot of arguing—but they never talked about the details.*

"*I'm not coming down if he's coming over!*"

"*You'll come down, Grandma. Dad is cooking mutton. There will be pie.*"

There was silence. "Pumpkin?"

"*Pumpkin,*" *Alison confirmed.*

"*All right, then,*" *she said, like she always did.*

Later that night, Alison broached the topic yet again. "When did you two meet? It had to be way before Dad was born," *she said, as her grandma was finishing off her second piece of pie.*

"It is impolite to ask a lady about her past," Grandma said primly.

"You and your 'lady' stuff," Uncle Nicholas said. He focused on the kids, a wicked grin on his face. He had long, wild white hair, and his hands were callused from years of building. He had kind blue eyes, and Alison had always liked him. "Ask her anything she doesn't want to answer and she'll say it's impolite to ask a lady that. It never fails."

Grandma Dia looked like she was about to hit him. "That is untrue. And it's impolite to spread rumors about a lady." Then she turned redder as the rest of them laughed. She dabbed her face with a napkin. "Your Uncle and I," she said, speaking directly to Max as if Nicholas weren't there, "went to school together. We had some of the same friends. He introduced me to your grandpa." She focused on Alison with this last point. "Which I admit I appreciated. But he's never been my favorite person."

"We have a pact," Nicholas said, winking. "There are secrets no one can ever know."

"What did I say about spreading rumors?" Grandma said. "Do not put ideas in the children's heads."

"I could tell them the truth," he teased. "Then they wouldn't have to wonder."

"You promised," she said sternly. She got up stiffly, turned her back to him, and said a polite goodbye to the rest of Max's family. She took her cane and gave a pointed look at Uncle Nicholas, then limped heavily out of the room. They heard her slow, plodding footsteps climb the attic stairs.

"Your grandma holds a grudge like you wouldn't believe," Nicholas said, watching her go. He smiled as he said it.

Max and Alison speculated, of course. Had they once been in love? Did he leave her at the altar? Were they secretly related?

They tried to figure out what kind of cousins they would be if Max's uncle and Alison's grandmother had gotten married, but it was too confusing.

"Doesn't have to be romance," Max said thoughtfully. "Maybe there was a cheating scandal at school and she covered up for him. Or she tore his blueprints and then he retaliated and shaved all her sheep."

"We'll probably never know. But I am sure that they were once best friends," Alison said. She'd seen the same amusement on Max's face when he infuriated her just for fun.

Alison shook her head to clear it of the memory as she approached Max. He sat on the bridge in the Hub, morosely swinging his dangling feet over the lava. Alison dampened her impatience and went to sit beside him. Idly she wondered if their shoes would fall off and burn away into the lava below, but that was possibly the least of their problems.

"When did he disappear?" she asked.

"Couple of weeks before your tree blew up," he said miserably.

"Couple of weeks," she said thoughtfully. "You mean around the time you almost drowned?"

He winced. "Yeah."

"I can't believe how you knew all along who we were looking for and you didn't tell me. And why isn't the rest of your family here, if he's missing? Why is this your job to do?"

He sighed and hung his head.

"You were right, you know: he's a terrible enchanter. It was his hobby, though. He loved it more than anything."

"That's not—" she started, but he kept talking.

"I wanted to learn from him but he wouldn't teach me, and my mom *really* didn't want me to learn. Said I needed to learn architecture instead."

"So you snuck out so he could teach you," Alison said. Max was pretty predictable.

"Yeah. He wouldn't let me try anything, though. So, one night I broke into his cabin and tried to test one of his enchanted helmets."

"The drowning!" Alison said, understanding.

Max nodded. "I thought it had a water breathing enchantment on it. Instead it weighed me down and I couldn't take it off. I barely survived, and they all thought I was dead. When I came home, Nicholas was gone. Mom said he . . . left."

Max's voice hitched for a moment, but he kept talking. "I went to the cabin and found it like—that. I tried to get as many of his journals as I could, but most of them were destroyed. I wanted to find him. Then your family, well, you know, then you came to live with us, and Mom wouldn't let me mention him, even when I told her about the cabin."

"Why didn't you just tell me?" she asked.

"What's more exciting, *I found a journal from a mysterious enchanter, let's figure it out,* or *My mother drove my uncle away after I took his helmet and almost killed myself with it, let's figure out the other stuff he's tried to invent?*" Max hung his head. "And I was afraid you'd tell my mom."

"But you didn't think I would tell her we were following plans from an unknown author who was far too fond of spider eyes?" Alison sighed. "You could have trusted me, Max."

"I know. I don't even know if he'll come back if we find him. Or if Mom will let him. She's still pretty mad."

"Does she know he's gone to the Nether?" Alison asked. "Surely she would be worried about him if she knew he was here."

"She doesn't even talk about him anymore. She hates him. Not only does she think he almost killed me, but after he disappeared, Dad had to move temporarily to the village to take over the big project Nicholas was working on. She blames him for everything."

"That's why your dad left. And why no one will talk about why," she said, realization dawning. Alison thought his parents might be somewhat justified in their emotions, but no one should be exiled from their family, and they definitely shouldn't be left in the Nether. "We could get him out of here, but we don't have to bring him back to your place. He can move. Better to live somewhere else in the Overworld than here."

"I don't know how to find him," he said miserably. "I didn't even know we'd gotten so close."

"Max, we weren't *close*. He beat us here by weeks. You lost, what, a few hours of that time from when we met Freya to now? Nothing is different, except I now know the truth."

They sat in silence, until Alison couldn't take the heat pricking her skin anymore. Uncomfortable, and irritated at their situation—and at her friend, who looked like he was settling in to feel sorry for himself for a good hour or two more—she stood up carefully on the bridge. "I still can't get over the fact that you pulled me to the Nether and you never told me why."

"I couldn't—" he began, not looking at her.

"No, Max!" she said, smacking his shoulder and making him look at her. "You could. Do you know why my parents died? Do you know exactly why they died?"

"The creeper—" he said, uncertain.

"No, it wasn't the creeper," she said. "Not directly. We don't have a lot of creepers around the farms and ranches, haven't you noticed they're mainly in the woods? Mom and I had a fight. She said there were some sheep lost deep in the woods, and she wouldn't let me go with her because of creepers. I told her I could handle it, and she said no. She said I was too young. I insisted I could help. I'd protected the sheep from wolves and zombies and stuff. I could deal with a creeper.

"I got upset and told her that I didn't need her anyway, and that I was going to live at your house instead. I left, but I just walked around in the woods for a while, feeling sorry for myself. When I wandered back near the house at sundown, I came face-to-face with a creeper. I panicked and *I ran*. I ran toward my house, then realized what I was doing, and ran past it instead. I heard it detonate behind me." She stopped, unable to speak for a moment. She took a deep breath. "I came back. The tree was mostly destroyed. Family were—gone."

"But that's not your fault," Max said.

"I led the creeper to the house. But that's not just it," she said. "My problem was, she was right. I wasn't strong enough to take on a creeper. And I keep wondering, was my sudden running away what triggered the creeper? I'll never know. But Mom told me I was weak, and she was right. And I hate that about myself."

"I'm sure she didn't mean—"

"Every time someone told me I wasn't ready for something, I was afraid they were right. But I didn't expect *you* to not have faith in me. We're stuck in the Nether and you didn't trust me to tell me the reasons why. Max, if you don't have faith in me, I don't have anyone left."

She got up then, and stalked away. Max scrambled to his feet. "Ali, don't. I'm sorry."

The door to the great hall slammed shut.

Freya walked up behind him. "What was that all about? Did you make up?"

"Not even close," he said, frowning at the door. "I think it's worse now. She's really mad."

"What did you do?"

He thought for a moment. "I . . . I don't think it is me, actually. Not this time. We need to let her cool off."

"Think she's going to the storage room for some food?"

Alison was in the great hall. Beyond that was the storeroom with the secret door—and beyond that, the Nether.

"No, I don't think she wants soup," he said, and went off at a run, then pulled up fast, grasping at his hip. "Oh no, where's Bone Bane?"

"Bone what?" Freya asked.

"My sword, my gold sword," he said impatiently. "I had it during the fight with the skeletons! It wasn't with me when I woke up. What did you do with it?"

"Oh right," Freya said, looking at his hip as if the sword were there and she just hadn't spotted it yet. "I think Bunny Biter may have taken it when she was cleaning the library of bones."

"You *think*?" he asked. "How can you not know?"

"I was preparing a healing potion at the time," she said, raising her eyebrows meaningfully. "Relax, I know where she hides bones. You keep an eye on Alison." She went off at a run back toward the library stairs. Max ran off in the other direction.

Please want some soup, he begged Alison mentally. *Just some soup. I'll even make it for you.*

The great hall enveloped him in heat and light when he burst through the door, but he ran on, wondering who in the world would want to have a grand meal in a furnace.

He got to the storage room door and closed his eyes, hoping to see Alison sitting at the table, angrily telling a bowl of mushroom soup how bad a friend he had been. He'd offer to listen instead and they would laugh. It would be a touching moment they could tell his mom about when they got out of this mess.

He opened the door and found what he had actually suspected: it was empty. The secret door was ajar, the torches flickering down the tunnel.

"Alison, come back!" he shouted.

There was no answer. Max looked impatiently over his shoulder to see if Freya had returned, and then rushed to the window. He wanted to run after Alison, but he was unarmed and knew he'd be next to useless without his sword.

Reaching the window, he looked out and saw a hole appear in the canyon wall; Alison stormed out. It felt to Max as if it were night, but the light remained the same bleak illumination coming from the lava and glowstone. At least there weren't any of those screaming fire creatures, Max thought.

Then a skeleton entered the canyon. Its head swiveled and its empty dead eyes stopped on Alison. It raised its sword and began walking toward her.

CHAPTER 14

WHEN NOT TO ACT RASHLY

When Alison had stormed away from Max, she could barely see past her tears. She had meant to get to the storage room, but she was too distracted by her own despair. She stormed through several doors and down a hall without thinking. Then she was outside.

She had decided to go back inside before she saw the skeleton; the arrival of the monster just cemented her resolve to get back to safety. The only problem was, there was a second skeleton behind her. She hadn't seen it when she'd stomped outside, and now it moved between her and the door.

Why does this keep happening? Alison stumbled backward, feeling in her pack for her bow. Her hand closed around her helmet first, and she fumbled it onto her head for a tiny bit of protection. Then she grabbed her bow, feeling the rough wood that indicated it needed some repairs. Would it last long enough to keep her alive?

The skeleton between her and the door raised its sword and began to hurry toward her. She raised her bow in return, knowing she'd be lost if it got within range of hitting her. She heard some clacking and remembered the skeleton entering the canyon. She checked over her shoulder and saw more skeletons coming in behind the first.

She turned slightly so she could see both of the first two skeletons out of the corners of her eyes. She took another step backward and loosed an arrow toward the closer skeleton. The shot went wide, and even more skeletons appeared. "I really hate it here," she mumbled.

An arrow whizzed by her cheek. So much for hoping they had only swords, then.

She headed backward toward the canyon wall, releasing more arrows, seeing some skeletons fall, but the satisfaction she might have felt was quickly dampened by the new enemies that took their place.

Life was more important than her pride, so she gritted her teeth. "Max? Freya? Help?" she called weakly.

The skeletons edged closer, swords raised. They were close enough that she could see their square eye sockets. Alison nocked another arrow and let it fly. The skeleton between her and the secret door fell, so she dropped her bow and made a break for the door.

She was too far from it still, and the approaching skeletons swarmed her.

Max, Freya, and the stupid thieving wolf ran as fast as they could down the secret tunnel toward the clacking battle below them.

"She can't take all those on herself!" Max said, wiping Bunny Biter's slobber off the handle of his newly recovered sword.

"I know that," Freya said, leaping over a mushroom patch in front of her. "That's why we're running."

From the outside drifted Alison's voice, calling Max's and Freya's names. She sounded far away and frightened. Max pushed himself to run faster. He snagged one of the torches from the wall with his left hand and gripped Bone Bane tighter. They had to make it in time, they just had to.

They burst from the secret tunnel just as Alison disappeared in a flurry of bones and swords. Max raised Bone Bane and shouted a war cry, but a light flashed from the middle of the skeleton mob and the monsters fell back, some of them falling down and twitching, then disappearing in a puff of smoke. Alison sat, stunned, in the middle of a circle of skeletons. She looked ragged and tired, injured but conscious. She wore the gold helmet she'd made for herself, the one that Max had tried to enchant. It was now glowing slightly.

Freya, Bunny Biter, and Max ran into the fray and made short work of the remaining skeletons. At this point it seemed easy, with Max keeping some at bay with the torch while he took others down with the knockback power of Bone Bane, and Freya's skill with her bow keeping the rest off them. Some of the smarter skeletons saw Bunny Biter and turned and ran.

Near the end of the battle, Alison had gotten to her feet, retrieved her bow, and taken down a few of her attackers. Most of her shots didn't land; her hands were shaking pretty badly.

The last skeleton fell with a clatter. The three of them stood, statue-still, while Bunny Biter began her customary clearing of the battlefield by grabbing bones, dashing inside, and then returning for more. Alison blinked at Freya and Max, said, "Your enchantment worked. I remember the journal called this one 'Thorns,'" and then toppled over.

Freya put her hands on her hips. "I swear, you two are going to drain me of supplies. Come on, let's get her inside." Carrying her between them, the two began the long walk up the secret tunnel. Bunny Biter ran at their heels, yipping muffled, joyful barks around a mouthful of bones.

from the lost journal of N

The merchants in the village are nothing but cheats. The woman
said I could have fermented spiders' eyes at a discount, but now
I can't find anything useful to put them in. I'm determined to find
the value of these things, as they must have one. Otherwise why
would someone go through the trouble of fermenting the disgusting
things?

So far, these potions do NOT work with fermented spiders' eyes:
 — Potion of Health
 — Regeneration
 — Night Vision
 — Swiftness
 — Strength
 — Water Breathing
I will keep trying, though. There's got to be _something._

(It will take some time to get started again because the Potion of
Swiftness with the spider's eye seems to do the opposite, and it's
taken me a full day to write this entry.)

Quit. I quit.

I know what my true path is, and I'm going to walk it. Let the others do the mundane work. I'm meant for higher things. Someday they'll be begging for my potions and enchantments. And of course, I will give it to them because I am not cruel.

But they'll know. And I'll know

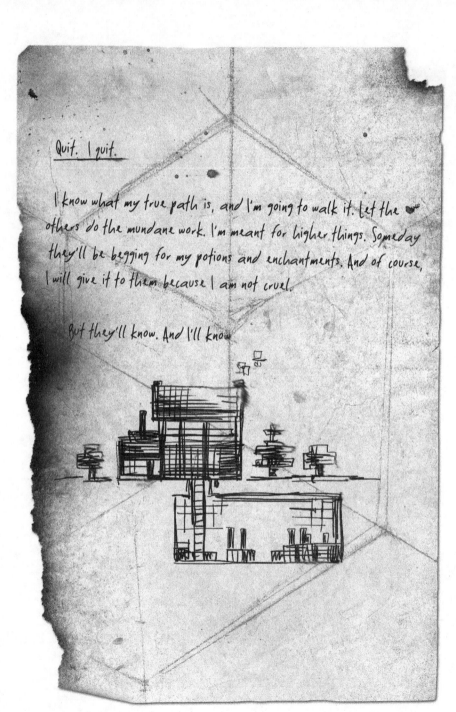

PART TWO

CHAPTER 15

MASTER ARCHITECT, FAILED ENCHANTER

Alison opened her eyes at last, smacking her lips and grimacing at the taste of the healing potion. "That's worse than mushroom soup."

Max didn't think it was that bad. He wouldn't go seeking it out if he was thirsty, but he didn't *mind* it. Alison looked like she had licked the underside of a donkey.

"What happened?" she asked, sitting up. Then her eyes got wide and tears filled them. She focused on Max, her lips trembling to make the words. "They're gone. And I can't bring them back."

Max had been prepared to defend himself against her rage again, but this was new and different and he had no idea what to do.

"Um—" he said, and looked over at Freya. She watched them with her arms crossed, standing a few feet away.

"I'm sorry I yelled at you, Max. It's not your fault. Just . . . everything hit me. I just wish I could make a decision about something in my life. But I just *react* to everything. Mom was right. I'm not ready." Alison pulled her knees up and wrapped her arms around them. She put her head on her knees and began to cry quietly.

"Hey, hey, it's okay," Max said, patting her awkwardly. "I'm, you know, not mad."

"Move over," Freya snapped, and pushed him out of the way. She wrapped her arms around Alison and held her until the tears stopped. It felt like twelve or thirteen years, but it probably was only a few days, to Max's estimation.

Alison looked up and sniffled, her face puffy. "Thanks. I'm okay now."

"Good," Freya said, and stood up. She went to a brewing station and tossed Alison a clean towel. "Clean yourself up. And then we need to talk about your helmet."

"Yeah, that's right, Ali," Max said, glad to be able to get back into the conversation. "It looks like I did enchant the helmet!"

Freya examined the golden helmet, turning it in her hands. "You were right, Alison, it's got a Thorns enchantment, so even though you dropped your bow, you still hurt them when they hit you. Then we saved your butt." She looked at Max. "That's about it, right?"

Max shrugged. "More or less." He would have liked to talk about how awesome he had been with Bone Bane, but knew he owed Alison more than that.

Alison looked like she was trying to remember. "Thanks," she said. "You didn't have to run after me."

"No problem," he said.

"Of course we did," Freya said.

"So, there's one thing I don't get," Alison said, wiping the tears off her face. "About your uncle, I mean. He's an architect, a really, really good one. What's with the enchanting? He's terrible at it."

Max sighed and sat on the floor, leaning against the wall. He wiped the remaining wolf slobber off Bone Bane. The blade had teeth marks on it from when Bunny Biter had tried to steal it.

"Well, you know Uncle Nicholas," he said. "The best architect in the family, he won a few awards for the ice castles he built in the north." He glanced at Freya. "Architecture runs in my family. Everyone does it. I'm expected to do it. Someone in my family has built most of the big houses in our village."

He looked back to Alison. "Did you know Uncle Nicholas designed your family's tree house?"

She looked startled. "No, I had no idea. Maybe that's why Grandma complained about it all the time."

Max smiled, remembering how the old people had constantly bickered. "Anyway, one night we visited your family for dinner. I remember he'd started to talk about a trip he'd taken in his youth, and your grandmother interrupted him and started talking about knitting and sheep. That made him mad. Later that night when we were walking home, Uncle Nicholas told me how architecture left him empty inside. How he'd had so much fun doing more exciting things when he was younger.

"He said he'd done some exploring with an archivist named Boots. They traveled around and Boots did the brewing and enchanting and he did the crafting and building. Boots wrote it all down. That was when he'd felt alive. He said he didn't have Boots anymore, so he wanted to do his own enchanting and alchemy."

Max studied his sword and decided it was clean enough. He carefully put it down on the floor in front of his feet and then sat back and looked up at the ceiling. "Mom got tired of his distractions. Said he wasn't doing his part of the family job. She and Dad had to cover the work he was supposed to be doing. When they found out he had been avoiding working in the village because he was building his enchanting cabin in the woods, they were so mad. They didn't want to hear that he was finally learning how to enchant stuff."

Max smiled sadly. "He was so proud. He would claim that he had enchanted things, but they were usually duds. His brewing was terrible, making explosive chemicals or just plain poison. But I didn't care. I loved his work. It was exciting!"

He sat forward and looked at the girls again. "No one got *excited* about architecture. I liked seeing him excited, and I started to get interested in enchanting instead of building. But my parents wouldn't let me see him after he moved from the village into the woods. So, I visited him when Mom and Dad didn't know where I was. He told me he'd enchanted a sword, but nothing else. I sometimes spied on him when no one knew I was there. I knew he was working on an underwater breathing helmet, and I watched him while he was enchanting it."

"That's why you thought it worked," Alison said. She looked at Freya. "He almost drowned because of his uncle's 'enchanted' helmet." She made air quotes with her hands.

Max nodded. "I broke into his house one night and got the helmet, then I went swimming in the river to test it. I got pulled down to the bottom, couldn't breathe, and blacked out. My family thought I was dead. I drifted downstream and someone must have fished me out and pushed the water out of my lungs. I don't remember much after that, but I staggered home. Mom and Dad were thrilled to see me, but at the same time they were yelling about Uncle Nicholas and how he wasn't allowed around our house, or even the entire village, anymore." He frowned as he remembered. "She wouldn't let me out of the house after that, and I had to stay in bed and recover, so I didn't know where he went."

Alison looked thoughtful. "I guess that would make this around the time of the creeper attack," she said. "I don't remember anything that was happening with you, except hearing you were okay after the accident."

He nodded. "Your parents' accident made my mom focus on someone other than me, which was great." He felt his face get hot with sudden shame, and looked away from her. "I mean, I'm not *glad* they're gone, of course, I just—"

Alison smiled sadly. "I know what you meant."

He relaxed. "Anyway, she told me he left town, but I went back to his blown-up cabin and found his journal and his notes. He'd left messages for my family, saying how sorry he was that he had killed me and how he couldn't face them anymore. And then I found the portal."

"He thinks you're *dead*?" Alison said.

Max nodded. "I was gone for hours. They all thought I was dead. By the time I was back, they were distracted by me needing healing, and then they were just so relieved I was back that no one went to tell him. Not like Mom wanted him around anymore anyway. Sometime around then, he built the portal, and shortly after that his cabin was destroyed."

"Which made you decide he was here," Alison said thoughtfully.

"And wouldn't come back home, yeah," he said. "I thought if I told him I was alive, he might come back. Of course, now I know he might want to come home, but lost the portal like we did."

She raised an eyebrow. "And you thought we could get him back? You, the kid who nearly drowned because of a helmet? And me, the kid who keeps attracting mobs like I am wearing some kind of skeleton lure?"

He set his jaw. "There was no one else. I started looking into the other journals and trying to figure out the things he made that worked, and the failed experiments. I tried to figure out who 'Boots' was, but I think they parted ways years ago. Then you came to live with us, and I figured I could use your help, and you could use a little distraction." They sat, silent for a moment, then Max added quietly, "He needs us. He thinks he's a curse on our family. He has no one else."

Alison sighed. "Okay, we'll find him and bring him home."

"He wasn't a curse, but it sounds like he sure made some cursed items," Freya said from the enchantment table.

"You're not helping," Alison said.

"Helped you, didn't I?" Freya said. "You both would be dead twice now if not for me."

"That's fair." Alison sat up and rubbed her arm where a sword had bit in an hour before. "So, what now?"

"What now?" Freya asked, annoyed. "What now is I get you two some reasonable armor and weapons so you will stop going outside in pleasant summer clothing! I didn't come here to spend all my time rescuing you two."

CHAPTER 16

UNNAMED HELMET

More mushroom soup. Alison gobbled it down, though. It seemed that nearly dying brought out her appetite.

"So, your house was built by his uncle, and then creepers blew it up, right?" Freya said, pointing her bow between Alison and Max. They were in the crafting room, Freya checking equipment while the two of them ate.

"More or less," Alison said. "My family raised sheep, mostly, but also pigs. Mom was an expert knitter. Dad made books that he sold to enchanters. Then, you know, the creepers, and—" She shrugged.

"Boom. That's what creepers do." Freya finished examining the equipment. "So, we have a gold sword here that was enchanted with the knockback enchantment," she said.

"Bone Bane," Max insisted.

"Do you know how long a gold sword lasts? It is a soft metal." Freya touched one of the tooth marks Bunny Biter had left on the blade.

"It's magic. It will last forever. And its name is Bone Bane," Max said through clenched teeth.

Freya rolled her eyes. She handed Alison the enchanted helmet. "This thing is also made of gold. What's wrong with iron, or diamond? Do you want to name it, too? Thorny or Rosey or something?"

"No thanks, I'm good," Alison said, accepting the shiny gold helmet that had saved her life. She knew most enchantments wouldn't stop an item from breaking. Max had better bring along a backup weapon just in case. And she should get another helmet, too.

"Come on, we need to get some more crafting done," Freya said, gesturing to Alison. She looked at Max, frowning. "If you want to try some enchanting on your own stuff, go ahead, but I'm not offering any of my equipment up for an experiment."

"Hey, I enchanted the helmet, didn't I?" Max said, offended.

Alison snorted. "Ask him how many failures we had," she said to Freya.

"Don't need to," Freya said. "Go get some metal out of that chest on the left. I figure we have enough diamond for each of us."

Max pulled his uncle's journal from his bag. "I need to figure some stuff out anyway," he said. He took a seat at a table next to a torch and held the journal up to the light, squinting at the angry, black scrawled designs.

Alison was starting to figure out that crafting was pretty easy, really, so long as you had the right amount of incredibly rare components. Crafting *equipment*, anyway. She wasn't going to mess with the magic stuff. She wasn't stupid. She had no idea how Max could keep messing with enchanting when it was so much more dangerous than crafting.

· · ·

Max had no idea how Alison could focus on boring crafting when enchanting was so much more exciting. But he couldn't do it without her items; he didn't have the patience or interest in finding the right amount of metal or crystal in order to make useful things. He was much happier searching for fermented spider eyes to enchant already-made equipment.

They made a good team, he admitted. They just should probably be more honest with each other.

He flipped through the book, his finger tracing the recipes he knew to be failures, and then the ones that he had figured out. He wasn't sure what he was looking for, but knew that the later pages, the ones with the heavy scrawled lines, held something he needed.

Behind him, Alison was working at her crafting table with great enthusiasm. Freya had given her a huge amount of diamond, which Alison had never even seen before, much less crafted with. She was happier than her sheep in the cove right now, and seemed to have forgotten they were stuck in the Nether with no chance of getting home.

He turned the page again and saw the thing that had constantly bothered him about this journal: there was one almost fully blacked-out page. He frowned in frustration. He had been unable to decipher what was originally written or drawn. What was he supposed to do with this? What was Nicholas trying to hide? He leaned closer to the book when he heard a "Whoops."

He was about to ask what had happened when a hot spark landed on his cheek. He yelped and jumped up, narrowly missing a sliver of hot metal that had chipped from Alison's work. It landed on the book and immediately started to smoke.

"Hey, watch what you're doing!" he demanded, forgetting the

pain in his cheek. He lifted the book and shook it so the burning metal fell to the floor, but the damage had already been done. A few pages had been loosened from their spine, and, combined with Nicholas's enthusiastic (or furious) scribbling, the pages were damaged enough to separate from the book and float to the floor.

"No!" he shouted, and went scrambling after the pages. Lucky for him, it wasn't windy in the Nether, and the pages settled on the floor gently. He scooped them up and held them out to Freya and Alison, shaking them slightly. "Be more careful next ti—" Focusing on the pages and now holding them up to the light, he realized that he could see more than when they had laid flat in the book. He put all but one down on the table and walked over to a torch, holding the page as close as he dared to the flame.

"What are you doing?" Alison asked.

"I thought I saw something," he said, looking so closely at it that his nose brushed the page. Beyond the dark scribbling he could see other writing, made earlier by a pen with a finer point. "I thought this was a page of failed recipes but it looks like . . ."

It was a map.

Alison didn't realize how stuck she'd felt simply because they hadn't known where they were going.

The lack of armor and the frequent injuries didn't help, of course, but those were barriers that they could overcome. But not knowing where they were going—that had been a burden on her shoulders that she didn't notice until they had a clear path.

Well, the path wasn't *clear*, exactly. It was still obscured by a lot of scribbling, but once Max had figured out the main lines of a map, and they realized where Freya's fortress lay in reference to the other things they could make out, they had a general direction they thought they could go in.

But first they had to get out the door, and there was a little issue stopping them. Max wanted to enchant his equipment.

Freya stood by the door of the basement, arms crossed, leaning against the wall. Max and Alison stood at an enchanting table, Max's new diamond armor between them.

Alison grasped the diamond helmet and shook it for effect. "We are in the Nether. We are looking for a missing man. You have a strong, new, incredibly rare set of armor. And you think that right now is the best time to start up enchanting again? It might ruin the armor!"

Max picked up his boots and shook them at her, mocking her movements. "Yes, I think now is the best time to do it. Are we ever going to need it more than now?"

"The way we're going, probably," Alison said. "Who knows what you're going to get us into next?"

Alison then counted off on her fingers the list of his failed enchantments, making Max's cheeks grow hot with embarrassment.

"But what about your helmet?" he asked, pointing to the gold helmet sitting beside her shining diamond helmet, armor, and boots. "I did that one right."

"True," she conceded, "but for all we know, that was a fluke. You have far more failed experiments than successful ones." Max dropped the boots with a clang and walked away from the table. He stared moodily at the tacky carvings on the wall.

Freya stretched, and Alison got the very annoying feeling that they were amusing her.

"Let's take the equipment we have," Alison said. "Max can

pack an enchanting table and whatever books and components he can carry."

"I can't enchant on the fly!" he protested.

"You can't enchant at all," said Freya.

"That's unfair and you know it!" Max said.

"Look, we're not trying to be mean here, Max; we're trying to save your uncle and survive in the Nether," Alison said. "We aren't in the woods anymore. This is serious."

Max relented with bad grace and packed up his enchanting supplies while Alison and Freya packed the health potions, food, and other equipment they'd need.

It was with sour moods that the trio left the fortress.

The Nether was strangely calm as they exited through the secret door. "Is this the best way to leave?" Max asked. "We haven't had good luck in this canyon so far."

Freya looked back. "The front of the fortress is always patrolled by blazes. You ever fought a blaze?"

He shook his head.

"Then we're leaving through the right door," Freya said. "Besides, we're stronger when we're together and no one is leaving in a huff completely unprepared for the mobs that await us."

"So, when we're all together, nothing attacks us," Alison commented bitterly as they stepped out into the dim Nether light.

"There is strength in numbers," Freya said, looking around. She had an arrow nocked, ready to protect them from any attack. The canyon was quiet, with only a few bones around that Bunny Biter had failed to find. She ran around now gathering them, looking at Freya, expecting her to open the door to the fortress tunnel so she could put them in her private collection.

"Not this time, BB," she said. "Pick your favorite and let's go."

The wolf blinked at her, bones in her jaws. She whined once, and then ran to Freya's heels, teeth clenched around the treasures she refused to give up.

Exiting the canyon, Max was finally able to look at the whole of the Nether without fearing massive mobs would overtake them.

The landscape unfurled before him, vast and brown, occasional gouts of flame bursting from the cracks in the ground. In the distance a red haze shimmered, looking like the lake that had been on Uncle Nicholas's map. Beyond that the world looked infinite, making him feel very small. Max remembered a desert his family once traveled through back in the Overworld; the sand and dunes went on and on, giving a false sense of safety in their monotony. They had seen nothing but rabbits and more rabbits. He'd forgotten that there were dangers other than mobs, though, and discovered what those were when he wandered away from his family. With no vegetation and no streams, he quickly ran out of food and water in the dry heat.

He'd underestimated the seemingly benign and bland landscape then. He wouldn't make the same mistake here. Even if there weren't terrifying mobs like those they'd already encountered.

They wandered around the corner to see Freya's fortress properly from the front, and she was correct: blazes still patrolled the area, throwing out an occasional fireball at each other, or random threats Max couldn't see, or imagined mobs. They were still a threat, however, and Max figured it would be good to keep his distance.

Freya looked at the map, which they had redrawn on fresh paper. They couldn't make out some of the areas, and Max had wanted to guess at what lay in those places, but Freya had refused.

"We'll map the areas when we get to them. Otherwise we'll get lost."

"We're looking for a lake of fire?" Alison said. "That's not narrowing it down."

Max pointed to the red glow that illuminated a hill in the distance. "I am betting it's over that way," he said.

Beyond Freya's fortress was the lava reservoir Max and Alison had initially seen, and beyond that was, well, another lake of fire. Only one of them was on the map, though, and Freya carefully added the other, estimating the number of blocks that the lava covered.

Max bounced up and down impatiently, his diamond armor clanking together. Although the only magical thing about him was his sword, he admitted he did like the look of the shiny armor.

Freya knelt on the warm ground and spread out two maps. "All right, from my own notes on this area, the land to the left of my fortress is barren with a bunch of mobs. I haven't gone right very much, mainly because there's what is essentially a lava sea in that direction." She pointed to similar marks on each map. "But from your uncle's marks, it looks like he went directly into the sea."

Max made a strangled noise. "Why would he do that?"

Freya glanced up at him. "I didn't mean that literally. I mean, he indicates that he wanted to go straight *toward* the sea. After that, who knows where he went? Maybe he made an under-lava vessel."

Alison put her hand on Max's shoulder and glared down at Freya. "If he were self-destructive, he wouldn't have worked so hard to come to the Nether. He was a master builder, Max. He's probably fine." She nodded toward the right. "We'll go that way, then."

Freya rolled up both maps and nodded. They started out,

sweat stinging their skin. The heat from the rock and lava was constant, and Alison wondered if they were going to die of dehydration before anything else. Now that they were out in the open, it felt both safer and more dangerous than the fortress. They were exposed, but so were all the other beings of this realm. Nothing could sneak up on them, and they took caution to stay clear of the patrolling mobs.

"What have you fought around here besides the skeletons?" Max asked.

"Don't forget those chicken jockeys," Freya said. "I haven't fought the blazes so much as dodged them and shot at them from a distance. There are scarier things than those, of course."

"Of course there are, because fire creatures aren't bad enough," grumbled Alison.

"There are the ghasts, and they're kind of strange. They throw fire a lot, which you'll see is a theme here. They're gray and a lot bigger than blazes. Four-by-four-by-four, by my account. They're so dumb that you can fool them into killing each other because even though they breathe fire, they're not immune to it. If they all shoot at each other, there might be one left over, but that one won't be a problem to deal with."

"Four-by-four . . . by-four?" Max said, looking around in panic to see if he could see the massive gray firebombs.

"Back in my fortress, we were lucky we only had skeletons in the library to deal with," Freya continued, nocking an arrow and looking around as they crested a hill of netherrack. "There are these cubes that like to hang out around and inside fortresses. Want to guess what they are made of?"

"Pumpkins," Max suggested, his voice indicating he didn't believe it for a moment.

"Fluffy wool?" Alison asked. Freya gave her a stern look. "All right, fire, they're made of fire, like everything else here."

"Exactly! Or magma, to be more precise. They've got a tough crust that's hard to shoot, and if they are big, they can just hop around and crush you. It's kind of cute from a distance, these red cubes just hopping around. You can kill skeletons and chicken jockeys, manipulate a ghast into killing its buddies, but it's best to just avoid the magma cubes. Trust me."

"Done," Alison said. "Totally believe you. I hope we never find out if you're lying to us or not."

"But you're lucky so far, because you haven't seen one of the worst things—"

Max and Alison interrupted her at the same time.

"Lucky?" Max yelled.

"The worst?" Alison said. "You haven't told us the worst one yet?"

"Yeah," Freya said. She paused at the top of the hill and looked around, her bow ready. Nothing looked ready to leap out at them. "The worst one is the wither skeleton, which can give you a wasting disease. We usually find several mixed in with a mob of skeletons, but I haven't seen any lately." She squinted down the hill, lowered her bow, and pointed. "That might be why."

On this side of the hill was a vast sea of lava, probably the one that Freya had warned them about. The heat coming off it was incredible, but when they squinted through the hazy air, in the distance they could see an island of netherrack. A massive tree of nether quartz rose from the stone, and within the crystalline branches sat a tree house made of Overworld materials. To the right of the house was a small-mushroom farm, with larger mushrooms growing on the left side. It was under these large umbrella-like mushrooms that the mobs swarmed. There were some skeletons, some zombie pigmen, but most were tall, blackened spindly things, like skeletons that had been stretched out and perhaps went for a swim in lava.

"Those are wither skeletons," Freya said. "They're all hanging out here. No wonder they haven't been bugging me lately."

"Uncle Nicholas," Max whispered.

Alison didn't say anything. She was too busy counting their supply of arrows.

CHAPTER 17

BOOKCASES IN YOUR BACK POCKET

Freya sat on the side of the hill, placidly watching the tree house for any sign of movement, human or mob-based. Alison paced back and forth, never taking her eyes off the island.

"So, there are the patrolling mobs that are possibly the worst in the Nether," Alison said, counting on her fingers. "The massive sea of lava with no obvious way across, and the fact that we're not even sure if your uncle is there. Is that all the terribleness in one fell swoop?"

"Sounds about right," Freya said. "Except you forgot the fact that we're also exposed here; and the more we focus on that island, the more vulnerable we are to anything else that might see us."

Alison whipped her head around to see if Freya was referring to any specific mob, but none of the monsters in the distance had gotten closer. Not too much closer, anyway. "Great. We need to find a way across, not fall into the lava, keep the skeletons from killing us, and hope that Max's uncle doesn't see us as a threat."

Freya laughed, her voice sounding flat in the warm desolation that was the Nether. "That would be something, if we got all the way over there, cleared out those wither skeletons for him, just to have him shoot us for trespassing."

"If by 'something' you mean 'tragic and terrible and tragic again,'" Alison grumbled. She looked around. "I keep thinking about all of us building a bridge," she said. "Where is Max, anyway?"

Max sat hunched over something a little way down the side of the hill. Alison hopped down a few blocks to check on what he was doing.

His armor was off and he was muttering to himself, picking up the diamond boots and then putting them back down.

"Max?" she asked, but he didn't answer, just hunched more. "Max!" she said in alarm.

He turned around, defiance scrawled all over his face. He jumped up and tried to hide the thing behind him, but it was easy to figure out. He'd taken out the enchanting table. "I figured it was time."

"You could get us killed," she said, rubbing her head with her hand. She was so tired of arguing with him.

"Do you ever say anything else? I might save us, too," he said, crossing his arms.

"Is he enchanting?" Freya called down the hill.

"Yes," Alison said.

"Does he know about the bookcases?"

She raised an eyebrow at him. "Do you know about the bookcases?" She wasn't sure *she* knew about the bookcases, but there was something apparently to be known. She knew that there always seemed to be a bookcase or three nearby enchanting tables.

She thought proximity to the shelves was handy because enchanting involved books, but there might be something else to it.

"I'm so far ahead of you I've already rescued Uncle Nicholas and we're back home eating pumpkin pie," he said, producing two bookcases from his pack and arranging them on either side of the enchanting table.

She sighed. Just give her a crafting table and a furnace any day. Enchanting was too troublesome. She watched him put his boots on the table and select a book from the shelf.

"I can't watch," she said, and returned to Freya.

"Hey, he hasn't blown up the hill yet," Freya said.

"He just got started," Alison said. "Do you have any thoughts about"—she waved her hand weakly toward the island—"all that?"

"You'll probably not be surprised that I have done a lot of research on lava since moving here," Freya said. "If Max can get us some protection spells going on the armor, I think we can make it."

"You're not suggesting we swim?"

"Sure," Freya said, getting to her feet. "I've got some potions of fire resistance. Max can enchant our armor." Alison raised an eyebrow. "All right, he can *try* to enchant our armor," Freya clarified. "Still, with those two things we can swim across that stuff with no problem."

"When did you brew those potions?" Alison asked.

"I did some when you were out, and had a stash of supplies for brewing long before you came vacationing here. Why does that matter?" Freya asked.

Alison didn't know why she was so frustrated. She frowned and walked away from Freya, who approached Max and peered over his shoulder. "Doesn't look like he's blowing things up this time," she called back, but Alison turned away and watched the red-tinged horizon and the floating terrors in the Nether.

She wanted to contribute. She wanted to do useful things like strategize and plan and make enchantments (or try to) and send a wolf into the fray.

Yes, she had made all of their armor, and upgraded weapons for herself and Freya, and that was useful. But now that they were in the field, she felt like all she was doing was telling them they were doing something wrong or dangerous. When had she become everyone's mom?

She remembered what her mother did when she got tired of being a mom. She would borrow a neighbor's horse and ride north to the tundra, bringing back white rabbit pelts and snow, and they would have snowball fights in midsummer. She said it made her feel alive, and like someone other than "just a mom."

When Grandma was tired of being an authority figure, she would throw her hands up in the air and yell, "Do whatever! I'm not your mother!" and then retreat to her attic space.

Now Alison was the mom, like it or not. She didn't want to be the mom; she wanted to be the hero.

"Alison, we're ready to test the armor," Max called. "I *think* it's got a fire protection charm, but there's no way of knowing until we get out on the lava."

"That's the only way you can think to test it?" Freya asked, punching him in the shoulder. "With all this fire everywhere, you just want to jump into the lava?"

Before he could answer, Alison decided it was time to act. She slipped out of her own diamond boots and tossed them to Max, who caught them in surprise. "Hand me yours," she said. "I'll test them."

His eyes grew wide. "Are you serious?"

"Yes, we need to get moving," she said, motioning for him to toss her his boots. "And you can enchant mine while I'm testing yours. I'm getting tired of sitting around here, let's do something!"

He frowned, and looked down at her boots, and then she was off down the hill.

Freya followed her. "Why the change of heart?" she asked from behind Alison.

"I said it. I'm tired of waiting. I'm tired of worrying. The worst thing has already happened to me, Freya. I lost my parents and my home. Then I got stuck in the Nether. What else is there for me to be afraid of?"

Freya glanced around. "I figured you were afraid of the Nether and the mobs and being stuck here forever, but I'm just guessing."

"Yeah, and?" Alison said, pulling on Max's boots.

"And . . . that's what I meant. Do I need to say anything else?"

"The mobs will be there whether I'm afraid of them or not. My fear doesn't affect anything except for me. And I'm tired of it. I'm so tired."

"I hadn't thought of it that way," Freya said thoughtfully. "You have a point. What's the point of being afraid?"

"Not that you can turn that off like a switch," Alison said, feeling her heart hammer in her chest as she approached the edge of the lava lake. The air was warm, but it didn't have the stinging, prickling heat that it so often did since she'd arrived here. "But it's good to realize you're just wasting time and effort."

Alison paused at the edge, one foot raised. She glanced back at Freya, who held a hand out. Alison took it gratefully and steadied herself.

Freya held her as she dangled one foot over the lava, edging nearer, waiting to catch on fire. But it never happened. The foot went closer and closer to the lava, and she could actually see the lava bow slightly as her boot neared its surface, as if it were trying to escape touching the boot at all costs.

"Do it," Freya whispered, and Alison plunged her foot in, her face screwed up in anticipated pain.

But she felt nothing. She could feel the resistance of the lava; this would be harder to walk through than air, or even water, but they *could* walk through it. For a short amount of time, anyway.

She pulled her foot out, shaking it slightly to remove the clinging lava, smoking in the air.

"You did it, Max!" she called. "It works!"

"No kidding?" Max called, sounding genuinely surprised. "Who would have thought I could do that?"

"You did!" Alison said. "Now, with your enchanting and Freya's potions we should have no problem getting there." She pointed triumphantly across the lake.

"Well, except for the mobs on the other side," Freya reminded her.

Alison firmly shook her head. "One problem at a time. My grandma used to say that you can't shear a sheep while you're repairing a fence. You'll get a fixed sheep and a shorn fence post." While she never learned what a "fixed sheep" was, she knew it made the adults laugh. Still, it reminded her not to switch her attention, and to focus on the most immediate thing. "Right now, we need to get across that lake."

Max and Freya joined her at the edge. "So, it really works?" he asked doubtfully.

"You enchanted the boots, you tell me," she said.

He shrugged. "Who knows what I enchanted them with?"

Freya handed each of them a vial. "Drink this right before you go in. It will last a while, but not too long."

"That's as precise as you can be?" Alison asked incredulously.

"We don't have clocks here," Freya said. "We work with what we have."

"So, we drink, and then we just walk into the lava and get across as fast as we can," Alison said. "Anyone have any other concerns?"

"Plenty, but no better ideas," Freya said cheerfully. She commanded Bunny Biter to sit, and then chugged the contents of her glass bottle. With a wink, she waded into the lake.

"And here we go," Alison said, and stepped in after her.

It was harder going than she had expected; lava was much thicker than water. Still, they could move through, and that was what they needed. "Just keep the cabin in sight," she said, wading deeper, trying to move as quickly as she could, jumping in case the lava was damaging her armor. The lava came up to her waist, and then her chest. Finally, she started to swim. It was strangely warm, and little puffs of smoke drifted up from their bodies, but she felt no pain.

The shore was drawing close, and Alison had already started trying to figure out their next move regarding the wither skeletons, but then Max started to scream from behind them, and things weren't so calm anymore.

In hindsight, it probably wasn't the best idea to ask Max what he had done wrong while he was still in the lava, screaming that he was burning. But she was going off instinct.

"Max, what did you do?" Alison shouted, turning around in the viscous fluid.

Max was jumping up and down, smoke wafting off him in bigger and bigger plumes. "It burns! It burns!"

"The potion should not have worn off so fast," Freya said in her ear. "But I don't think his enchantment worked on every piece of armor."

"We didn't test every piece!" Alison said, horror dawning on her. "What do we do?" She looked from Freya's calm face to Max's panic. She saw flames flare on his armor, and knew he would just get more and more hurt as time went on, unless they acted.

"Grab his shoulders," Freya said, and before Alison could yell *"What?"* in disbelief, she had disappeared, having dived *under* the surface of the lava.

Max rose slightly from the lava, and Alison realized Freya had grabbed his legs. She took his shoulders and held him above the lava, while Freya surfaced, his ankles in her hands. He was heavy, but between the two of them they could carry him, and they hauled him, still burning, to the edge of the lake.

Freya dropped his legs, and Alison dragged him the rest of the way onto dry land. She pulled his still-smoking armor off, noticing with alarm the burns that were covering his body. Unfortunately, his smoking boots and helmet would not come off, no matter how hard she pulled. At some point she had to admit she was part of the problem, causing him pain as she tried to wrench the burning armor off him.

Freya rushed over with another vial in her hands, this time a potion of healing.

"I don't think I did a good job enchanting this time," he said weakly, choking the potion down.

"You didn't drink the potion, did you?" Freya asked, taking the empty vial from him.

He relaxed back onto the rocky ground and closed his eyes. "I thought the enchantments were enough and we should save the potion."

"So you botched the enchantment *and* failed to drink the potion?" Alison said incredulously.

Freya put her back to them, bow raised, waiting for the mobs to discover them. "He's paying the price," she said over her shoulder. "And that armor's not going to come off."

Alison bit back her further raging. Freya was right. She checked out his burns. "You'll be okay, though, it looks like the one health potion will be enough." She looked at the remaining vials of healing potion. "We should save these."

Max lifted his head from the ground. "Save it? Why don't you save me?"

"The fact that you can complain about this means you're probably fine, Max," Freya said, not looking at him. "Besides, we need you right now."

"Need me for what?" he asked, grumpily sitting up. His clothes had stopped smoking, and he was no longer radiating unbearable heat while she stood next to him, something she had noticed as her own heat protection potion wore off.

"That," Freya said, raising her bow. They had come onto the island at the closest tip, which was unfortunately the place where the giant mushrooms grew and the mobs gathered. The mobs were starting to take notice of the trio, edging closer and then stopping.

"Why are they just standing there?" Max asked.

Freya took a step forward, squinting in the low light. "Your uncle needs to stick to architecture," she said, smiling.

"Why?" Alison asked before Max could argue.

"Because he's trapped them in some kind of glass box."

It was true. The mobs were encased on all sides by glass blocks, having the ability to stare out at the kids, but go no farther. The zombie pigmen milled about the prison, oinking occasionally, but the other mobs just silently watched them.

"They can't break through, right? If we don't get near them, we should be fine?" Alison asked.

"I'd feel better if they all were dead," Freya said. "No surprises."

"We can't take them all on!" Max said, struggling to his feet. "Not with nowhere to run! If they're not going to bother us, why risk it?" He pulled at his helmet, grimacing. "This thing is cursed," he grumbled. He glared at Alison.

What did she do? It wasn't her fault. Then Alison realized he was waiting for her to say, *I told you so.* She smiled sadly, turning away from him. She was remembering how her mother would always be the more levelheaded of her parents, and never would rub it in anyone's face when they turned out to be wrong.

"I don't like leaving them just milling about there," Freya said, frowning. "These are nasty mobs." She considered the pigmen. "Well, most of them."

"Better reason than any to stay away from them," Alison said, nodding to Max. She realized it was the first time in forever that they had agreed on something. It felt nice.

They heard a strangled bark from the other side of the lava lake. Bunny Biter was trembling in her sit, clearly wanting to come to the aid of her master. But Freya had commanded her to stay, and she was a good wolf. It didn't keep her from sitting still and barking furiously. Clearly she didn't appreciate being left behind.

"Oh, dang wolf," Freya said, sighing. "I told you to stay!" The wolf barked once more, and then howled.

The wither skeletons began to rustle more, and the pigmen

edged away from them. Alison tried to figure out how tough that glass prison was.

"You go knock on the door," Freya said. "I'll stay here to keep an eye on the dumb wolf so she doesn't do anything stupid, and watch those mobs for you."

Alison and Max looked at each other once, united at last in their plan. Max put on the non-cursed parts of his armor, gave a tug at the stuck pieces just in case, and then sighed. They walked around the perimeter of the large mushrooms, keeping well out of the way of the wither skeletons, who stared at them from the shadows.

The tree house was a work of beauty. Alison felt a pang that it was in such a terrible place; it was a house worthy of royalty. A ladder stretched up the trunk of the obsidian pillar, leading to a porch and the front door. The manor itself sprawled through the crystal that grew in all directions. Small rooms connected by crystal corridors were hidden throughout, and Alison wanted nothing more than to explore the entire thing.

"This is amazing," she whispered to Max as he mounted the ladder. "Do you think your Uncle Nicholas would let us have a tour before we take him home?"

"That's what you're thinking about right now?" Max said, looking down at her. "Unbelievable."

"It's a nice house!" she said hotly, and followed him up the pillar. "Don't tell me you don't want to explore it." From the porch, they could see farther in the reddish glow of the Nether. They could see mobs wandering on the horizon, and distant lakes of lava. Bunny Biter barked from her side of the lake, outraged at being left out of the fun.

"Fancy houses don't impress me, remember?" he said. "I've

seen plenty. Although this does look like Uncle Nicholas's work. It's not like any of the fortresses we've seen."

They walked toward the door. "Are you ready for this?" Alison asked.

He shrugged. "Ready for what? I'm just going to tell him I'm alive, and it's time to come home."

He turned from her, and she let him have his confidence, no matter how brittle that confidence was. He walked up to the door, his hand raised to knock, and he froze there.

Alison walked up behind him to see what he was staring at. There was a folded note attached to the door with two words visible:

GO AWAY.

CHAPTER 18

NOT A USELESS SKILL AFTER ALL

"It looks like he doesn't want to be found," Alison said from over his shoulder, and Max felt his rage spike.

"That's obvious!" he said hotly, ripping the note from the door. He knew he shouldn't blame her, but he had to blame someone or he would go mad. He looked around wildly. "Is he spying on us? Why doesn't he just show himself?"

He stomped to the edge of the porch, the note clutched in his hand. He glared into the distance, hoping to spot his uncle hiding somewhere nearby, even amid the wither skeletons under the mushrooms.

"Do you want to see inside the house?" Alison asked from beside the door.

"You really want a tour right now? We have to go after him!" he snapped.

"I was thinking of looking for any clues he may have left behind. At the very least we might find some supplies. We need to get back across that lava, remember," she said calmly. "But it might be dangerous. We don't know how long he's been gone."

"So?" Max said.

"We don't know what has spawned in there in the meantime."

"I'm pretty sure he put any spawn areas under those mushrooms, which is where those things came from." He waved down at the giant mushrooms. "It's something he would have done."

"Doesn't mean there can't be more inside," she said.

"Oh, do I have to do everything?" he snarled, and brushed past her to push the door open.

A crash sounded behind them, but Max couldn't turn and see what had happened. He was frozen in fear, his eyes locking with the purple, blank stare of the enderman hovering just inside the door.

"Run!" yelled Alison, wheeling around and grabbing Max's hand. She jerked him back just as the tall, lanky, black creature began to scream. Three more clustered behind it, and Max of course had to look at all three before allowing himself to be pulled away.

They rushed to the end of the porch, and Max had the wild idea to jump, but figured the fall or the lava would finish him off, so he turned quickly and slid down the ladder, Alison ahead of him. She jumped out of the way when she landed so he wouldn't pile on top of her.

The endermen were waiting for them when they got down to the bottom. Max had forgotten they could teleport.

"Freya!" Alison called. "We need those potions!"

"And some help!" Max added as he took a swipe at one of the endermen with his golden sword. It teleported away easily, popped back next to him, and hit him with its arm. He felt the armor take the blow, but it knocked him backward, and he stumbled to catch up with Alison.

"Freya!" he called in desperation, and he saw his friend not paying attention to them at all, but dashing in their direction, wither skeletons and the once-docile pigman mobs enraged and pouring out of a hole in the prison behind her.

"Freya what did you *do?*" Max asked. "They weren't bothering anyone!"

"I was mining some blocks, accidentally saw an enderman, it hit me, I fell into the glass, the pick broke through, I accidentally made a hole. I must have hit a pigman because they got mad. So I ran." Once the trio was together, Freya switched their direction, leading Max and Ali toward the edge of the lava lake. "Bunny Biter, come!" she shouted, and the wolf was at her side with a joyful bark. Max wished briefly that crossing the lava lake could have been that easy for all of them. Freya stopped at the lava's edge and started putting blocks of netherrack at the edge of the lake. "Max, do you have any mined blocks with you?"

Max thought quickly, taking stock of what was in his bag. "Yeah, some, why?" he asked.

Alison caught on before he did. "Make a bridge? Why not just get back the way we came?"

"Max has cursed armor, we don't have much fire protection potion left, we can't fight while we're in lava, and we need to get moving *now,*" Freya said. She looked at Max. "Alison said you were good at building on the fly?"

He nodded, understanding. *Oh, they want a tower for safety! That's what they're talking about.*

"Yeah, I can do that!" Max said, and started grabbing granite blocks from his pack. He tossed one on the ground and then another one on top of it, then jumped onto the short stack. He jumped up again and placed another block under his feet.

"Build OUT!" Ali shouted, pointing at the far shore. "Build a bridge, dummy!"

Max cursed at himself and modified the direction he was moving in. Building out quickly was harder than building up, but with the threats behind him, he was inspired. He angled himself just right and placed a block down, pushing forward. The girls jumped up behind him, covering the rear, as he built three blocks high over the lava.

"Alison, with me," Freya said. They took guard positions behind Max to keep the mobs off them. Max was placing blocks as fast as he could, moving out onto the lake as his bridge got longer.

"Alison, aim for the hole, get the ones coming out. I'll get the free ones," Freya said.

"Got it," Ali said grimly.

Max turned to see Freya shoot an arrow at the closest enderman. It teleported away, which he expected, but when it disappeared, the arrow skewered the enderman directly behind it. It took the arrow full force, staggering backward.

"That's one way to do it," Ali said, sounding impressed.

Now that he was out over the lava, creating a bridge two blocks wide, he had vivid memories of a short time before when he was in the lava when the fire protection wore off. He slowed down, placing the blocks a little more carefully. He ran out of granite and switched to dirt, not daring to look in his pack to see how many blocks he had left.

An enderman teleported beside him, and Max nearly leaped back, which would have been a disaster for him, Freya, or both. But he remembered where he was—and what was all around them—and stood his ground. He planted his feet and swiped at the enderman with his sword, and it flailed backward and into the lava, where it twitched once and teleported away.

"It won't try that again," said Max, grinning. Then he stopped grinning. Bone Bane, his precious sword, clattered down and skidded to the edge of the bridge. He reached out for it, but then saw that it had broken. *I guess gold wasn't as strong as I'd thought.*

He chanced a look back. The panicked pigmen were milling about, no longer a threat, but some of the wither skeletons had pushed through the pigmen to pursue them. They joined the kids on the bridge, chasing them down.

"I think I'm going to need that sword of yours, Max!" Alison called, loosing arrows at a mad clip. The skeletons were still getting closer.

"I do too!" he said. "But it's gone."

"Gone? What do you mean?"

"Gone! Broken! No work anymore!" he said, and looked in his bag to see if he had packed any backup weapons. Then he froze. The only things in his bag were a pickaxe and the note he'd found on the door. Not only did he not have spare weapons, he didn't even have any more blocks to build with.

He thought fast. They were only a few blocks' distance from the shore, but he knew even a little time in lava could be the end of him. "Freya, I'm coming back toward you, but I'll stay low."

"All right," she said, still sounding calm even with death screaming behind them, and sizzling under them. She adjusted her stance as he got down on all fours and crawled up to her feet. The mobs were only about a dozen blocks away, and closing fast even with the girls shooting down the ones in front.

"I need more blocks," he explained as he chopped away at the bridge between them and Nicholas's island. "We might need to make this narrower."

"I guess you're good with balance?" Freya said, scooting to the right when Max took the block to her left.

"I'm great at it," he said, "but I've never tried it over lava." The dirt block he had just removed crumbled and fell into the lava with a hiss.

Freya stowed her bow and took out a diamond sword. She handed it to Alison. "He needs help," she said, and got out her own pick. She made short work of a block of granite and tossed it to Max. He caught it, embarrassed. "Let me dig, you build," she suggested, and he nodded, cheeks burning.

Alison furiously swung the diamond sword, thinking she'd much rather have her bow. But Freya had been right; this was better for close quarters. She held off the mobs, swinging to keep them away more than damage them. She knocked a few pigmen and wither skeletons into the lava. The pigmen squealed and disappeared, the wither skeletons just glared at her. They couldn't reach her now, and she couldn't kill them with lava, so they were at an impasse.

The endermen she just waved her sword at. She couldn't have hit them anyway, but at least she could keep them out of range.

Behind her, Freya and Max had narrowed the last five blocks of the bridge to just one block wide, and added the blocks they'd removed to the end, bringing the bridge closer to shore. They still weren't close enough. "Now what?" asked Freya, directly behind Alison.

"Take the bridge away," Max said. "Then they can't follow us."

Alison took one more swipe at a wither skeleton and jumped backward, switching to her bow when she landed. She kept shooting as Freya bent down to take the block of the bridge that Alison had just vacated. They worked that way, with Alison shooting and stepping backward toward Max, Freya taking the block from under her feet and tossing it to Max, who slowly built them toward the shore.

"Will the endermen follow us?" Alison asked.

"I don't think so. They got distracted by the lava and the other mobs, just like I'd hoped," Freya said. "Bunny Biter didn't hurt either."

Max got the bridge two blocks away from the shore and jumped to safety, tumbling to the ground, exhausted as his adrenaline gave out. The girls fell beside him, Bunny Biter teleporting in from Max-didn't-know-where, but she carried a stone sword between her teeth and looked very pleased with herself.

"Let's not do that again," Alison said, panting and staring into the red sky and rubbing her right wrist. "That wasn't fun at all."

Most of the enemies had disappeared due to the rain of arrows, or had fallen into the lava, and those that hadn't had returned to the island. The endermen wandered the shore, teleporting to and from the tree house porch, acting as if the three kids hadn't even been there at all.

"So, how was the visit with your uncle?" Freya asked.

It hurt Alison to see Max's face when he saw the note was actually meant for Freya. But what did he expect? Nicholas thought he was dead. Still, Max paled and frowned when he saw Freya's name at the top of the note, and then handed it to her wordlessly.

She read it aloud:

Dear Freya—

<u>Don't follow me.</u> I appreciate your kindness when you rescued me, and I'm sorry I left you without saying good-bye. But I'm a cursed man, hurting everyone I come across. I came to the Nether because I was responsible for my nephew's death. I don't deserve anyone's kindness. I can never make up for it so I'm taking my exile as far away as I can. So don't follow me farther, it's just going to get more dangerous.

Nicholas

"It sounds like he won't come with us even if we do find him," Alison said, grabbing the note from Freya. "Hey, you didn't finish reading. There's a P.S. here."

P.S. Also, I worked hard to build this house, and was pained to discover it immediately got infested with spawning mobs. So, don't come inside, there are endermen and skeletons likely wandering the house.

"Oh," Max said. "Maybe we should have read that note first."

Alison couldn't help herself. She started to laugh. Then she grimaced. "I think you should look at something for me," she said to Freya. "I didn't think it was a big deal, but . . ."

She held out her right arm, showing her wrist where it peeked out of her armor. There was a wound there; it wasn't a deep, worrisome cut, but even a shallow cut shouldn't look black and puckered around the wound.

"Did one of the wither skeletons hit you?" Freya demanded, pulling Alison's armor off so she could get a better look.

"Yeah, but it wasn't a bad cut, I barely felt it. It was right after I'd removed that last block to give to Max. I didn't think it was—"

"—a big deal, yeah, you said," Freya said, frowning. "That was a *wither* skeleton, Alison. Don't you understand what that means?"

"I'm starting to get an idea," Alison said, fighting the urge to rub her arm again. It ached deep into the bone, and she was experiencing a weariness that felt much deeper than it should have.

Freya rummaged around in her pack. "One more fire protection vial. Two more healing potions. A few others . . . No, I don't have any."

"Any what? Why not just give her the healing potion?" Max asked.

"Because that would be a waste. It would make her feel better but not heal what's hurting her, and she'd get sick again and then we'd be out a potion," Freya said impatiently.

"Milk," Alison said softly.

Freya nodded. "Yeah, milk will negate the effects. But I don't have any on me, and cows aren't really found wandering in the Nether. Not even mooshrooms. I may have some back at the fortress."

Max glanced back at his uncle's tree house. "I guess going back to see if Uncle Nicholas left any behind would be suicide."

Freya glared at him as her answer. "We can go back to my base, and lose whatever ground we've gained on Nicholas, or we could go forward and hope he has a solution once we find him."

Alison glanced down at her arm. "How long do I have?" Her eyelids were drooping.

Freya examined the wound again. "I'd say about half a day," she said.

"I need rest," Alison said. She lay down with her head on her pack and closed her eyes.

"No, no, Ali, we gotta get up. We only have half a day, like she said." Max put his hands under her armpits and heaved her to her feet. She grunted in annoyance.

"Come on, Ali, you can do this," he said. Freya got under one of her arms on one side and Max took the other, but she shook them off. Max was right. She could do this.

After a few hours, they all took a rest. Ali dozed off immediately while Max and Freya studied the letter for more clues.

"What do you think it meant that he is taking his exile even farther away?" Max asked. He was settling Ali's head on his pack to make her more comfortable. "What's farther than the Nether?"

Freya glanced at Max as if to gauge whether he could handle the truth of what she was about to say. "It's not *quite* the farthest you can go," she said. "There's one more place beyond here. It's called the End. It's where the endermen come from, and the ender dragon. It's hard to get there, and even harder to get back."

Max rifled through Ali's pack, a mushroom stem sticking out

from his mouth; he chewed on it thoughtfully. He grabbed more mushrooms for Ali to eat when she woke up. She'd need her strength. Well, she really needed milk. But food would have to do for now. He felt distant and sad, as if he weren't a part of this journey anymore. It had become too big for him.

"Uncle Nicholas never did anything halfway," he said. "He built the biggest houses when he didn't have to. He wanted to learn all the enchanting and alchemy recipes, even though architecture was plenty. He left the whole of existence when he thought he'd killed me. It wouldn't surprise me if he left for as far as he could go."

"We'll find him," Freya said. "We just have to hope we get him before he builds another portal. Because I'm not going to the End. I can take you to your uncle, but if he's already traveled there, you're on your own."

"I thought you were in this with us," Max demanded.

"To get back from the End you have to kill the ender dragon. And you saw how a few endermen and skeletons nearly got us killed. How will we handle a dragon?"

Max stared at her.

She shook her head again. "If you find him, I'll help. But if we find a hot end portal, I'm heading back home."

Max went to sit beside Ali, ready with the mushrooms when they would have to get her up and moving again.

From the lost journal of N

I think we can communicate with the endermen. They want the same things we do: they want to be left alone, have no one look at them, and to teleport anywhere they like. (Note: They are actually able to teleport, while at this point it's only something humans _want_.)

I have tried to communicate while not looking at them. I offer food, blocks, useful tools. I try to speak, or grunt, or scream, but they don't seem to care about me until I look at them, and then things get ugly again.

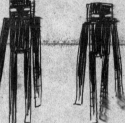

I've tried to watch the endermen together, to see how they interact, but their lives seem to be relatively solitary, yet often with companions.

I hear the endermen come from a place called the End, and that it's harder to get to than even the Nether. I will go there someday, but I must finish my excursions to the Nether first. Boots always said to be thorough.

Put in another bookcase today. It turns out that enchanting is easier with more book cases around. Almost as if the books are drawn to the enchantment. Which makes sense since you need books to enchant.

Have discovered that it's harder to enchant things with just any book. I used the popular novel My Heart Is Square to enchant a helm, and now I have an iron helmet I can't take off. In the woods that's fine. In the village I tend to stick out.

The book was pretty good, though.

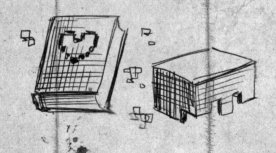

PART THREE

CHAPTER THREE

CHAPTER 19

THE WRONG WAY

Alison woke up when Freya poked her gently in her good arm. She winced; her other arm felt like dead flesh hanging from her body. She poked at her wrist, her elbow, and then her upper arm. She missed the pain; that had at least meant it was alive. This numb feeling was worse.

"Well, you woke up easily enough," Freya said. "How are you doing?"

Alison tried to shrug, but only one shoulder responded.

Freya bent down and examined Alison's arm, her face doing a terrible job of hiding her worry. Alison felt nothing when Freya explored the wound, wiping it clean with a cloth. "This doesn't look good. We need to find some milk, now."

"But what about Nicholas?" Alison said, struggling to her feet. She looked around and realized that it was only the two of them. "Wait, where's Max?"

"I assume he's looking for milk," Freya said, going through Alison's pack and moving some of the heavier things to her own.

"We took a quick nap, but when I woke up he was gone." She frowned and sat back. "Maybe he thought we were dead weight. Maybe he went ahead without us. Maybe he got eaten in the night. I don't know."

Alison squinted at the girl and realized she was angry with herself for letting Max get away. She looked around at the unfamiliar landscape. They'd left the lava lake and Max's makeshift bridge behind. "I don't even know what direction to go in now," she said. "Did he take your wolf, too?"

Freya sighed. "I don't know that either. Bunny Biter sometimes wanders off, but she always comes back. I don't think she would have left with Max, but maybe she wanted to protect him. I just don't know." She pursed her lips, like she hated saying those words.

Alison put her own pack—thankfully lighter now—over her good shoulder. "Let's head off that way," she said, pointing. "Maybe we'll find Nicholas, or Max, or your wolf, or a friendly stranger with some milk. Sitting around here won't do us any good, regardless."

Freya focused on her at last. "I figured you'd be more upset about everything."

Alison smiled sadly. "There's not much left to lose. Sitting around won't help us find anything. If we move, we have a chance. Just keep your bow ready. I can't help out with fighting anymore." She winced, but was grateful that her shoulder still had enough nerves to cause pain. "Let's go."

Freya took one more look at the horizon, and then they headed off to the next destination on the map.

. . .

Max wasn't aware of how much time had passed. He had been focused entirely on finding the milk for Alison, but multiple distractions had bothered him.

First, he realized that he could return to Nicholas's house so long as he didn't look at the endermen, and so long as he kept away from the wither skeletons. There were a lot fewer enemies now; the girls had taken care of most of them. He kept his head firmly focused on the ground as he took the bridge back over the lava, supplementing the holes with netherrack he'd taken from the hillside.

He heard the skeletons clacking in their shady hideout by the remains of the glass prison, but didn't get close enough for them to take interest. He saw a wispy black form here and there while walking, but didn't look at it. He climbed the tree house carefully, still looking down, and then pushed open the door, looking the other way while he did so.

Nothing happened.

He walked inside the house, trying to see out of the corner of his eye if any mobs were waiting to pounce, but the house looked clean. The upper level looked to have a living area with a table and chair, some books and bookcases, and some chests with very little inside, mainly wood and some coal. Max made a few torches and ventured down the back stairs to a workspace on the back of the house.

Nicholas liked basements. He had filled this one like the cabin in the woods, with a few workbenches, a brewing stand, and an enchanting table. Bookcases lined the walls, interrupted occasionally by chests. Max chose a chest at random and opened it. So many beautiful weapons were inside! Diamond and gold weapons, glittering and urging him to take them. He had to go and tell Alison and Freya; this was too good.

Alongside the weapons was a set of simple leather armor, folded neatly and looking as if someone had placed it there quite by accident and would be back for it.

It had to be specially enchanted! With all of the supplies his uncle had here, there was no way he would waste time enchanting leather armor unless he meant to put a really special enchantment on it that no one would guess.

Max dropped the diamond armor Alison had made for him, donned his uncle's leather armor, and went rummaging through the rest of the stuff.

He didn't find anything else worthwhile, but right before he left the room he spotted two books behind an enchanting table. He snagged them and saw they were more journals, leather covers feeling newer, less handled than the journal he now carried. Nicholas must have left them behind by accident when he'd vacated the house in a hurry.

Max ran his fingers over one cover, identical to the other journal with a circle surrounding the two dots, and opened it.

I know he watches me while I'm enchanting items, and I know his mother doesn't know. I've seen the boy follow me, he is so sure of his stealth! I would laugh except then he would know I had uncovered his secret.

The feelings are complex when I sense his presence at the window. My heart swells with pride when I think that perhaps he wants to follow in my footsteps as an enchanter, and not the rest of the family's legacy as architects. But he will have seen my mistakes so many of them, and then I wonder what he must think of me!

I know what his parents think. Rose has told me time and again to not encourage any interest that he may show to my "hobbies," as she calls them. They want me to do nothing more than show him the skills I have as an architect, and leave him to a life of boredom. But they haven't seen the boy build yet; he lacks the family skill. Oh, he's competent enough, he can build a sturdy wall, floor, or bridge, but the boy has no vision when it comes to architecture. His houses will keep people warm, but their visual appeal will be negligent.

But enchanting! His eyes light up when he thinks he's seeing a magical item, and his hands visibly itch, he's so eager to get a hold of the item. I've seen him pore over books, not understanding half of what he was reading but being entranced by all of it.

Next week I plan on telling Max I know he's been spying, and I will train him in secret. With his enthusiasm and my tutelage, he may become the best enchanter this world has ever known!

If we are careful, Rose need never know.

I can't even read my previous entries, as I know they drip with pride and confidence. This failing of mine, this pursuit of such a dangerous vocation, has killed my nephew, and it is more damning that I knew he was watching me work, that I didn't stop him, or at least let him watch where I could see him and we could talk about the dangers of enchanting.

He broke into my cabin and took a helm I had attempted to enchant with a water breathing spell, but had failed. His complete faith in his uncle had him drown, and when I heard, I ran, my sister's cries of anguish behind me that I had killed her boy.

I had such dreams for him, having no child of my own I had wanted to give my nephew my world, my legacy, my knowledge. I had hoped to take him with me to the Nether and show him it isn't the hellscape of legend, that it can be a fascinating place to visit. Now I exile myself there alone, with nothing left in this world but pain.

Max could read no more through the tears in his eyes. He hadn't known this about his uncle. Nicholas knew he was a terrible enchanter but he knew Max watched him. He had wanted to train him!

Max's face had flamed hot when he read about his "average building skills." He had tried to get more innovative, but had never really risen to his parents' expectations. But Nicholas had never cared.

He shook his head and took a deep breath. He tossed the journal he'd just found into his pack and opened the second one, which contained fewer personal entries and more recipes. He lost himself in the pages of Nicholas's plans for testing other enchantments. His uncle had thought he could make flame-retardant clothing in order to allow people to visit the Nether and be safe. He wanted to calm endermen so that humans could visit their villages and hold peace talks. He'd had plans to give Max a saddle for his birthday that would allow him to tame any riding beast. His enchantment ideas went on and on, from the completely mundane-but-useful, like a window that was black on one side and clear on the other so that a creeper or skeleton couldn't post themselves at your window and watch you, to giving you the outrageous ability to fly above the Overworld, never take falling damage, never encounter a monster, and always find whatever vein of metal you needed for your projects.

Max chuckled, wiping some stray tears from his cheeks. Nicholas always had the strangest ideas.

I am exiled.

I've made a new home here in the Nether.

I found another young person who may have looked up to me, but I abandoned her. I can't be the cause of another child's death. She reminded me so much of Max that I had to leave.

I have tried architecture here, building a grand treehouse much like I had in the Overworld. It immediately became infested with mobs. I can hear Boots laughing at me now. She's telling me she's safe and happy and I'm a fool for coming back here.

I'm leaving the new place and searching for an existing fortress to capture for my own. Someday I may find my home in the End, but for now I only want to find a safe place to lay my head, and this is not it.

"He's not going to the End," Max said softly. "He's looking for a home here." He sat down on the floor, the armor digging into his back, and, Ali forgotten, read further.

CHAPTER 20

MAX'S MOM TAUGHT HER BOY POLITENESS

Max's eyes were dry and burning. He blinked furiously, surprised he didn't hear the lids closing like sandpaper sliding across the marbles in his skull. How long had he been there?

He jumped up. *Ali.* He had come in here to find help for her and ended up on the floor going through his uncle's things. He felt confident he knew where to find his uncle now, or at least the general direction, but what about Ali?

Cursing the lack of light and not being able to tell how much time had passed, Max got up and stretched. He would feel better if he could take his armor off—if only the chest plate and armored trousers—but they wouldn't budge.

He pulled and pulled, shouting angrily as he realized in a panic that his uncle had cursed these pieces just as Max had cursed his own helmet and boots. Now he had a full set of leather armor that he couldn't take off, while his vastly superior diamond armor lay on the ground.

Stunned at his own lack of sense, he carefully picked up the diamond armor to take with him. He searched the remaining chests, picking up whatever potions looked useful, but looking for milk specifically. He finally found some, in Nicholas's kitchen area, of course, and got as much as he could carry.

With the old armor, the new potions, and the new journals, he dashed from the house, avoided looking at the endermen (although he did bump into one and say "Excuse me"), outpaced the skeletons and the pigmen in his haste, and ran back across his recently repaired bridge, barely feeling the heat from the lava lake.

He crested the hill and kept running, looking for their camp, but slowed when he realized he didn't see any sign of his friends. Had they broken camp and moved on without him? He looked around frantically, wondering how they could have abandoned him; he hadn't been gone that long. Had he?

He had to admit to himself they didn't know where he had gone either, and possibly they were off looking for him. Still, his planned save-the-day entrance was ruined now, and that made him grumpy. He ran to the top of the hill to his left for a better vantage point.

He spotted her, then. Netherrack had been excavated to build a small shelter, and an even smaller person lay inside. It had to be Ali. He ran down the hill, clanking in his cursed boots, heavy pack banging against his body as he ran.

Lava gouts burst up from the landscape as he went, and he had to dodge to avoid them. It felt almost like the Nether itself didn't want him to get to her. He wondered if the lava could burn the cursed armor off his body, but figured that might be a very bad idea. Might as well cut his arm off because he got a bruise.

While Ali had been visible from the hill he had been on, once he reached the ground she was obscured by some mushrooms and smaller hills. He ran around them, worried that losing sight of her would mean losing her all over again. But when the shelter was in sight again, he could still see the figure resting inside. Heartened, he tried to run even faster.

Now that he was closer, he could see the figure was definitely Alison, and she was resting with her armor beside her. A movement caught his eye: Freya was running on his right, Bunny Biter at her heels, heading for Ali as well.

They reached the tent at the same time, and both started breathlessly talking.

Max said, "I went back to Nicholas's house to see what he had in there, and found a bunch of weapons and armor and two more journals, and I think I know where Nicholas was going! He's looking for a fortress like yours to live in, and I think I know the direction to go in. I lost track of time but I got a bunch of potions and some milk!"

At the same time, Freya said, "I found that fortress you saw on the map and I think that's where Nicholas is going, but it's guarded by a bunch of skeletons. There was a blaze and a few docile pigmen too, and this massive lava fall, but Bunny Biter showed up and we got through it, but it's too complicated to tell you how. Needless to say, we don't need to feed her for a few days. But we also found a cache of items that included milk!"

They ended up saying "milk" at the same time, and looked at each other, startled and annoyed. They started accusing each other of abandoning the other, and demanding to know where each had gone, since neither had heard a word the other had said. Then they finally noticed Ali.

She was very pale, looking up at them with shadows under her wide eyes. She looked as if she had lost weight already, with the wither sickness wasting away her body. "The milk?" she asked.

"Oh, yeah," Max said, fumbling at his pack. He and Freya produced canteens at the same time, and Freya held Alison's head up while Max poured the milk down her throat. She coughed and spat and drank some more, then they eased her head back and waited anxiously.

"How will we know when it works?" Max asked, glancing at Freya, who had dropped her easygoing manner; real worry creased her brow.

"I don't know. I've never cured wither before," Freya said. "I expect she'll tell us."

"Can't we give her some healing potion and see if she gets worse again?"

Freya shook her head, but Alison answered for her: "That would be a waste of a potion, if the milk didn't work. Just wait . . ."

She closed her eyes and sighed, and after a moment said, "And stop staring at me."

Max and Freya exchanged glances again and stood up, walking a few steps away from the shelter to let her rest.

"Why did you leave?" they demanded of each other at the same time.

"I wanted to find help!" they both answered hotly.

"Yeah, but I *really* wanted to find help," they said.

They lapsed into silence, Max afraid to say anything else she might be able to anticipate. Finally he said, "I'm sorry I lost track of time."

"And I'm sorry we didn't leave a message for you," Freya said. "I was just so—"

"—worried about her. Yeah," Max finished.

"I just hope we're not too late," they said in unison again, and gave each other weak smiles.

"So, we both figured out where Uncle Nicholas is probably staying?" Max said.

"If it's the same fortress, yes, but I don't know if he's inside. I think there's a good chance." Freya looked back toward where she had run in from. "I just don't get why he left that tree house."

"He said the monsters spawning drove him away," Max said, digging out a journal and handing it to her. "But fortresses spawn all kinds of monsters. He's not going to find anything different in an already-created house."

"There's one thing a fortress may have that's not going to be in any house he creates," Freya said, looking excited.

"Well?" Max said, not wanting to take the bait, but eager to hear the rest.

"I've heard that some have portals to the Overworld within," she said. "It's possible he is looking for that."

"Do you think he wants to come home?" Max asked. He hadn't wanted to voice his concern, but one very real fear he'd had was finding Nicholas and being unable to convince him to return to the Overworld.

"We won't know until we find him," she said. "I think once he finds out you're alive, then that might help."

"Then let's find him," said a voice behind them. They turned and saw Ali there, still looking rough around the edges, but clearly much better. They whooped, and Freya tossed a healing potion to her, which she fumbled and dropped.

"Just give me a minute," she added, picking the vial up off the ground and uncorking it. "Once I'm back to normal, we'll find him."

CHAPTER 21

MORE BREAKING AND ENTERING

Alison had thought Freya resided in the most amazing and complex fortress she had ever seen, and now it may as well have been a shack. The fortress they suspected was Nicholas's was built atop thirteen pillars of nether brick, suspended over a lake of lava. The base was wide and fortified with an obsidian wall, but they could see the upper floors peeping out from behind the wall. It spread out like a plant in the Overworld, with incomprehensible towers jutting up from flat rooftops, balconies overlooking the lava lake, and what appeared to be a greenhouse on the left side, which made little sense with no sun.

It was probably well-lit by the lava fall that cascaded down a cliff farther to the left, actually.

Just in case the skeletons and hopping magma cubes patrolling the shore of the lava lake didn't deter you from investigating, the "bridge" going to the fortress was made of blocks of obsidian ascending to the base of the fortress. Each "step" was one solid block: no railing, no stairs to make climbing easier.

They would have to jump up each one and hope they didn't fall into the lava.

They stood well away from the fortress, where the mobs by the lake wouldn't notice them. Alison gazed at the walkway to the base. She was feeling much better, but her legs still felt shaky. "I'm really tired of lakes of fire," she said. "Does this place have anything else? How about a friendly garden? Or an unfriendly garden? I'd give anything for a spider-infested forest right now."

"It's the Nether, Alison, not a snow biome," Freya said. "We have two kinds of landscape here: lava, and not lava."

"You have mushroom plots too," Max suggested, polishing the very-unenchanted-but-much-stronger diamond sword with his back to them. "And soul sand."

Now that Alison was feeling better, she noticed that Max was looking decidedly different. "Why are you wearing that armor, Max? Did the diamond already break and I didn't notice?"

He turned around, not meeting her eyes. "I found this in Uncle Nicholas's tree house in the crystal. I thought it was enchanted. It . . . well, it *was* enchanted. Cursed, really."

Alison's mouth fell open. "You mean *every piece* of armor you're now wearing is cursed? And you took off solid diamond armor to wear leather armor that you can't remove?"

He flushed. "Yeah, I know. It's terrible. I'm stupid. I should have grabbed the milk and come back to you guys. Anything you were going to say to me, I've thought of it already, believe me. But there's nothing I can do about it. Maybe I'm cursed with this stuff forever." He shrugged, uncomfortable.

Alison smiled sadly. "You're not stupid. That armor is a connection with your uncle. I think I'd grab any connection to my family right about now. Even one of my mother's garish banners."

Even an enchanted terrible banner. We'll get that off you some-how, just, you know, be careful."

"It could be a good opener for a conversation when we find him," Freya suggested. *"Hey Uncle, guess what, you didn't kill me, but oh yeah, I'm stuck in this awful armor you made, can you help a guy out?"*

Max surprised himself by laughing alongside Alison and Freya, trying to imagine Nicholas's face when he told him he was here to rescue him and, by the way, he also was wearing a full suit of cursed armor.

Alison sobered. "I'm not sure there's anything we, or even your uncle, can do, though. That's why it's a curse. It's on you until it is destroyed."

He grimaced. "And anything that destroys the armor is likely to kill me soon after it falls off, right?" he asked.

"Probably," Freya said, nodding. "We could just dip parts of you in lava until the armor burns away and then pull you out really fast. That might work."

Alison had an image of holding Max by his feet over a lava pit, trying to burn off the cursed diamond helmet, and shuddered. There had to be a better way.

Freya crossed her arms and focused on the skeletons. "I've been trying something with Bunny Biter," she said thoughtfully. "I think it might help us out a lot." She gave the wolf a pat, waking her up. She'd been sleepy since her adventure with the pigmen and the blaze, and Alison suspected she had a very full stomach. Bunny Biter looked up with an inquisitive whine.

"Bunny Biter!" Freya said in a commanding voice. The wolf jumped to her feet, alert. "Sic tibia!"

The wolf was off in a flash, heading for the skeletons. "They'll tear her to pieces, she can't take them all on!" Alison said.

"Relax, if it all goes south then we run in and help," Freya said.

Alison fumbled for her bow. It would have been nice to know they were about to fight. She was still trying to figure out how to get the cursed armor off Max. She nocked an arrow and aimed at the mobs.

The white wolf was still running at full speed, heading for the nearest skeleton. It noticed her and tried to back away, but the wolf was closing in fast. The other skeletons noticed the commotion and started clacking away from Bunny Biter.

"Freya, this was a bad idea," Max said, raising his sword, but Freya put a hand on his shoulder.

"Just give her a minute," she said, watching intently.

The wolf reached her prey, but she didn't leap and attack. She darted in low and clamped her powerful jaws around the skeleton's lower leg bones and yanked. The startled menace flailed as it fell backward, taking another skeleton down with it. Bunny Biter shook her head once, snapping the leg off, and then ran off, the bony foot flopping on the end of the leg as she ran. The other skeletons followed this new, strange threat at a safe distance, shooting off the occasional projectile at her, while the de-legged one rolled around, trying to get up and failing. Freya almost leisurely put a few arrows into it, and it disappeared, leaving behind a bow and a bone.

"Will she be okay?" Alison asked, watching the wolf lead the skeletons away.

"She's faster than they are. If she gets hurt, she can eat the leg she's carrying. She'll be fine," Freya said. "Come on." She and Alison started forward.

Max heard a whistling in the sky, and grabbed both girls' arms and pulled them backward.

THUD. A very large cube, black with red eyes, and radiating more heat than even the surrounding area, landed where they had just been standing.

"Scatter!" Freya cried, and took off away from the lava lake. Max and Alison followed.

"What is that?" Alison yelled.

Freya looked back at her with wide eyes. "It's a magma cube. And don't run with me! *Scatter!*" Without warning, she cut to the right, running in a completely different direction. Alison chanced a look backward, but didn't see the menacing cube anymore.

She slowed, which probably saved her, because the cube landed in front of her with another thud, throwing her off her feet with the force of its landing.

She hit the ground and rolled, the heat of the monster wafting off in waves. She really didn't want that thing touching her.

"Why can't we meet anyone nice?" she yelled, climbing to her feet. The cube launched itself into the air again and she watched its trajectory, then ran forward, passing under it so that it landed behind her.

Max appeared by her side, holding his sword. "You okay?" he asked, his eyes on the cube.

"We need to split up," Alison said. "That thing will crush you without good armor, don't get under it!" She dashed off in a new direction, pulling her bow from her pack and hoping Max took her advice.

"These things look like slimes," Max said, crossing her path to run the other way. He kept talking over his shoulder. "Fire slimes, anyway. I bet they'll break apart like slimes!"

Alison ran for a few moments, and then heard Max whoop in triumph. She risked slowing down and looking for him.

The cube was gone. Around Max now were four smaller cubes. They looked just as scary, but more manageable even with their greater number.

"It worked!" Max yelled as the group of cubes split up. Two of them came for Alison, one hopped tentatively toward Freya after spying the spot she had taken on a hill to get a better shot with her bow, and the last one jumped toward Max as he swung his sword at it.

"Keep it up, they'll keep breaking down," Freya called, raising her bow for a shot. "Stay alert."

"Who's falling asleep?" Max asked, swinging again and catching the cube in mid-jump. This sword didn't have a knockback enchantment, but it was clearly a much better weapon. It sliced right into the cube and then knocked it sideways. He hadn't split it fully, and now it was bouncing and heading for him again.

Alison's bow was just a plain old bow; diamond could do nothing to make that better. So she shot an arrow at the closest cube, hitting the right spot but the arrow bounced off the cube's tough crust. If she couldn't pierce it with an arrow, how was she going to fight it?

Freya was stronger than she was, and the cube pursuing her had several arrows sticking out of it. With one more, it shuddered, bounced backward, and separated into four tiny cubes.

Alison didn't have time to watch them and figure out how they could fight the tiny ones, but Freya didn't look so concerned now. Max was running toward Alison, but the two cubes heading for her were way ahead of him.

She thought fast, and pulled her pickaxe from her pack. She quickly dug a hole a few blocks wide and two deep, and then stood in front of it.

"Come on, take the bait, I'm just standing here, begging to be squashed by you," she muttered. Both cubes leaped again, sailing toward her. As they fell, she jumped away at the last moment.

It worked, partly. One of the cubes fell into the pit behind her.

The other one got lucky and landed on the edge of the pit right beside her. It glared at her, trembling. Alison realized it was getting ready to jump again, so she kicked it with her diamond boot. It fell into the pit, colliding in midair with the other cube as it tried to jump out. They both tumbled and hit the ground inside the pit, and Alison leaped forward with netherrack cubes at the ready.

With one quick motion she filled in the hole, trapping them before they could jump out. She could hear their frantic thumps as they jumped and hit the ceiling of the chamber she had created.

She threw a few more netherrack blocks on top just to make sure they would stay in there, then stood back and sighed in relief.

Freya was stomping on the tiny magma cubes, but Max was ignoring the ones he had created.

Alison raised an eyebrow and pointed at the tiny bouncing fire cubes trying desperately to follow Max. "Are you going to clean up your mess?"

"I was going to ask if someone without cursed boots would help me out here," he said. "I don't think it's a good idea for me to go around stomping on *magma*."

Oh. Alison ran forward to finish stomping out the mobs. Her enchanted diamond boots didn't even register the heat she was stepping on.

Once more she worried about Max fighting in cursed armor. How long would he be forced to wear this, and would he survive if it fell off in the middle of a fight?

Freya joined them and looked around. The area near the fortress was quiet, for the moment.

"It's clear. Let's go."

In the other buildings they had explored, Max and Alison had found all of the crafting and enchanting areas in side or basement rooms, almost as if Nicholas (and whoever had occupied Freya's fortress before she did) wanted to keep the crafting and enchanting a secret. This place, though, put creation front and center.

The room that, in another fortress, would have been a ballroom or a great dining hall was the crafting room, with furnaces, crafting tables, and the usual run of creation blocks they were now used to. They opened a few of the chests, which were much emptier than those in previous places they'd visited, which was disappointing, although they did find a few blocks of obsidian in one.

"Not enough to make a portal," Max said. "Maybe he's off looking for more, so he can come back and finish it?"

"We don't know for sure this is your uncle's fortress," Freya reminded him, looking around the room. "This could belong to someone else. Or your uncle is somewhere in the building; we haven't looked through the whole thing. Maybe he got hungry. He could just be in the kitchen eating some ender steaks."

"Is that . . . a thing?" Alison asked.

Freya looked at her pointedly. "It should be," she said.

Ali turned slightly green and dropped the topic. She left the room, muttering something about checking the rest of the wing of the house, and returned shortly saying that no one was in the kitchen, but she was happy to report a few cauldrons of fresh water. She looked less green and more refreshed.

They went through the remaining chests, although no one donned any of the few pieces of armor they found, with Max's cursed items as their example of the consequences of being too eager with loot.

Two chests did hold much more exotic provisions than the others: supplies Max and Alison had never seen before, like boiling tears, small living flames, and the creepiest thing Max had ever seen.

Alison opened one chest and jumped back with a yell. She edged closer and peeked inside, Freya and Max coming up behind her.

A huge green eye peered out from the chest at her, looking around the room, focusing on Alison, and then checking out the room again. "What is that?" she asked.

Freya looked in the chest, and then at Alison. "It's an eye," she said slowly.

Alison glared at her. "Fine. Then what is a giant green eye doing— No, wait." Freya would tell her the eye was just looking around. She rephrased the question. "Why is there a giant green eye in this chest, and what is it used for?"

Freya grinned at her, looking as if she wanted nothing more than to take Alison literally all day, but they didn't really have that kind of time, so Max spoke. "I've heard of magical eyes that can find strongholds in the Overworld. I don't know if this is one of those, or if it can do that down here."

"Well, since we're in a fortress, it would find the one we're in and call its job done, wouldn't it?" Freya asked. She peered over Alison's shoulder. "Is that all that's in there?"

"There are three of them, and that's it," Alison said, frowning in disgust and stepping back. "Let's look in the other chests. I don't want anything to do with those things."

They found several books and enchanting tables. Freya and Alison glanced at Max, and then at their as-yet-unenchanted equipment. Max looked up eagerly. "I'm game to try it if you are!" he said.

Freya shook her head. "We've got too much cursed armor already. Experimenting now will just cause more pain and suffering."

"I need to practice if I'm going to get better," he grumbled. He wandered down the rows of bookshelves as he sulked, trailing his hands along the spines of the books.

"All right, we've got ourselves a fortress, we need a missing uncle, and then we keep looking for a portal. Or more obsidian. Want to guess where the uncle might be?" Freya asked, walking to the window of a tower room where they had discovered three enticing-looking beds. Or death traps, as Freya called them. Considering that sleeping in a bed in the Nether would cause deadly explosions, these beds were an insult to their backs, which were sore from sleeping on the ground.

Max suddenly realized he would gladly take any punishment his mother wanted to dish out to him if he could just sleep in his own bed again. His homesickness hit with an unexpected punch, and he wondered how his mom was dealing with their absence. How long had they been gone, anyway? She must be so worried. *She'll never let me leave the house again.* He sighed, his breath shaky. They'd get through this. They had to. He had to get home.

Alison looked at the beds with the same longing as Max. She tore her eyes away from their deceptive welcome and joined Freya at the window. "Well, we could stay here and wait for him to come back. Maybe he was waiting on someone—"

"Some*wolf*—" Freya corrected.

". . . wolf, right; he was waiting for the monsters to go away, regardless," Alison said. "Speaking of which, where is that wolf?"

"She'll be back at some point," Freya said, but her focus on the outside landscape showed her concern.

"We should go out and look for Nicholas," Max said. "I can't stay cooped up in here waiting for him."

"He has a good point," Alison said thoughtfully. "Then again, if you're out there fighting while wearing cursed armor, that's not very good protection."

"I'll be careful," he said. "You're not a hundred percent better yet; it doesn't make sense for you to go and me to stay. And if we all go, with our luck, we'll leave and he'll come back here. Or we'll stay here and he'll be out there, dying of a wither cut or drowning in lava or something."

"Then we split up," Freya said. "Alison stays here and waits; you and I go out and make sure the path to the fortress is clear." Her eyes almost gleamed in the low light.

"I'm game to stay here. There's plenty to read. But how can you go looking for a fight right now?" Alison asked, sounding weary.

Freya shrugged. "It's about all I do. Hunt mobs. Find food. You guys showing up has given me the most variety of the past several months, honestly. And the three of us are still hunting mobs."

Max brushed off his cursed armor. "Let's do it," he said. "Then we can find your wolf when we go out."

"There's a bonus," Freya agreed, but Max could tell she was relieved to not leave Bunny Biter out there on her own.

They helped Alison set up torches throughout the hallways and rooms she thought she would be using while they were gone, lighting the areas to avoid attracting monsters, and then checked their equipment and supplies.

"You got some good stuff at your uncle's," Freya said, going through his inventory. "Healing potions, protective potions, more milk. I wonder why he didn't take this with him."

"I think he left in a hurry," Max said. "He also left a few journals behind. But hopefully we can ask him when we find him. Come on, the day isn't getting any longer."

"Actually, it's always day here," Freya said. "So it's not getting any shorter, either. But I'm ready." She slung her pack over her shoulder.

Alison waved at them from her place at a crafting table, where she was engrossed in a book. "Be careful out there. This book says there are some pretty nasty mobs."

"What are you reading?" Max leaned in close, peering at the cover. "A journal by 'Leocadia'? What kind of name is that?" Max asked. "And are you telling me there are things out there nastier than what we've already met?" Alison shrugged and didn't look up from the book. "Anyway, don't burn down the place while we're gone," he added.

She grinned up at him. Max and Freya closed the fortress door behind them and looked over the red landscape. Max was getting tired of this scene, always low light, always red and heat-shimmery. On the horizon, a few skeletons pursued something, their weapons raised. Max pointed. "I think that's as good a place to start as any."

Freya checked her arrow supply. "Then let's go."

Notes from 1000 Terrible Creatures and Why You're Not Permitted to Find Them Under Any Circumstances

By Leocadia Stiefel

Entry 1

I don't understand the point of this, making notes about an absolutely terrible place no one should ever visit. But I suppose children don't like to hear "don't go there." They need to hear exactly why one shouldn't travel to this terrible place. And that's why I have come here, to find all the reasons my children—or anyone—should not travel to this "Nether."

I am here also to keep my companion safe, despite his constant poor jokes and his insistence on giving me a ridiculous nickname. But he asked for protection, and I am here to give it. A lady is nothing if she is not a reliable friend.

We arrived, by my estimation, yesterday, and immediately encountered three reasons to go straight back home. Fire, lava, and ghasts.

Ghast (pronounced "gast"): Screaming like a newborn baby is the sound you will hear to alert you to a ghast's proximity. These four by four monstrosities fly around, dangling tendrils beneath them, looking for someone to attack with their fireballs. They're lazy creatures, wanting nothing more than to sit on their couches and wait for their wives to make dinner.

I'm kidding. That was my first husband. They reminded me of him, however. Ghasts simply sit around and use their fireballs' considerable range to attack from afar. It's rare they will travel to attack, but it can happen, so you can't sit around and lazily think you're fine if they're at a distance from you. I hate laziness.

They're easy to dispatch if you can avoid getting hit by their fireballs. Their bodies are fragile bags, easy to puncture with an arrow or even a fish hook.

Drops: Why someone would want tears from such a creature I certainly don't know, but they do drop their own tears, which I know is a trick to make me feel sorry for them, but it will not work, thank you very much.

Oh, and the tears can be used in potions. I suppose they can be useful that way.

PART FOUR

CHAPTER 22

THE GRANDMOTHER JOURNAL

Alison marked her place in the journal as she watched them go, wondering if their plans would work out or if they would discover that Nicholas was gone for good. She was beginning to lose hope, although she'd never tell Max that. But how long were they going to search for him?

Max was wearing all cursed armor, she'd nearly died from a wither skeleton attack, and they kept finding enticing and dangerous crafting areas designed like they were meant to trap them and encourage them to make bad decisions.

She crossed her arms and looked at the great crafting hall with skepticism. This land was beyond inhospitable and had many rules that were downright deadly for no apparent reason. Again, she found herself really wishing there weren't tempting beds upstairs; at this point she might lie down on one, because even if she exploded, she would at least die comfortable. And *why* were there beds upstairs? Whose idea of a sick joke was that?

This was not the best way of thinking, Alison conceded, and

she started taking inventory of the chests again. Against her better judgment, she started with the creepy chest full of eyes. She opened it and took out the top one. She knew it wasn't a "real" eye; this was smooth and cool like a stone, and not squishy the way she would have expected an eye to feel. It was green and shiny, and looked around the room as she held it.

"Now, what are you for, little eye?" she asked aloud, but it didn't answer her. If it had, she wouldn't have been surprised, not after the days she'd been here in the Nether. But it merely looked at her.

The precisely written journal might tell her.

She'd found it in the bottom of a chest, reminding her of Nicholas's journal while being wholly different, in that it was clearly and carefully written.

She shuddered and put the eye on the table beside the journal, and flipped it open again.

The handwriting was painfully neat, in a way that made her hand ache to think about making such careful letters. The whole thing was methodical and orderly, almost obsessive, its pages crammed with as many words as possible. She read slowly to make sure she didn't miss anything.

The eye of ender is a rare and sought-after item that you may sometimes find within treasure chests, but rarely. If you're a fighter (and you definitely should not be one, I hope I raised you better than this), you could craft one, since crafting one requires an ender pearl, something that's easiest to get by killing an enderman. "Easiest" is a joke. My companion says I don't make enough. But endermen don't take kindly to people looking at them, much less killing them and taking their pearls, so I suggest finding the eyes, or finding the pearls and mixing them with blaze powder. The powder is also difficult to get, but if you're out hunting endermen then you might as well hunt a few blazes and get their loot as well.

Really. You're better off finding an eye than crafting one. If I find out you've been hunting components to make this item, you will be punished.

Once you have your eye, whether looted or crafted, it's more than just a knickknack to bring out at parties to creep out your hosts. (I admit to doing this in my youth, but I now regret it.) In fact, we recommend you not do this because someone at the party might know what you have, and may try to take it from you. And if you're a thief who loots chests in homes that don't belong to you, then you deserve what's coming to you.

Where was I? Ah yes, the eye. Its uses. It can do two frightfully useful things. One is to build an ender chest, an amazingly convenient storage item that allows you to access anything in the chest from any other ender chest. How the chests know not to get your items mixed up with the other users of the chest, I don't know. That's not my job. I just know it works.

The eye of ender is also a key of sorts, allowing you to build a portal to the End. The eye of ender is a key from a world you would never want to visit to a world you should never go to. But whatever, it's your life, go ahead and do stupid, weird stuff with the eyes in this box. I won't be around to see all your bad decisions.

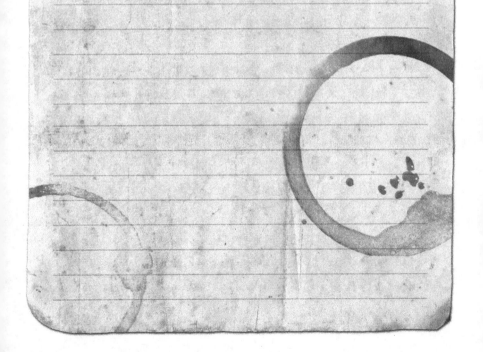

"It sounds like Grandma Dia could have written this," Alison said aloud, laughing.

Then she quieted. Realization washed over her.

The text was informative, snarky, and a little passive-aggressive. Concerned with doing the right thing and being a lady, and very stern. It certainly *felt* like her grandmother. But Grandma Dia had never been to the Nether.

But she knew Uncle Nicholas. And Uncle Nicholas had traveled to the Nether several times in his youth.

He'd said his expedition companion was named "Boots." Not Leocadia Stiefel.

Leocadia.

Grandma's name is Dia.

Her mind raced as she turned the journal back to the beginning and read the opening, this time imagining Grandma Dia's voice as she read the words.

How was this possible? Alison felt dizzy as she wondered what in the world had made Grandma Dia travel to the Nether with Uncle Nicholas, back in the day before their families grew.

She returned to the journal.

On page eight, Nicholas was named. On page twelve, she admitted that her hated nickname was "Boots," since that's what her last name meant.

Grandma Dia had changed her name when she'd married Grandpa Robert, long dead.

It was all coming together.

"What would you have done if you'd known your old friend had exiled himself to the Nether?" she whispered aloud, wishing her grandma were here so she could ask her. She missed Dia, and the rest of her family, badly at that moment, and slid the journal away from herself, trying to get ahold of her emotions.

A *lady doesn't spend her time adventuring around*, Grandma Dia had said after Alison came home one day covered in scratches from wandering through the woods with Max. *But if you are going to decide to not be a lady, always prepare yourself with the proper tools.*

Her throat tightened. Grandma Dia hadn't been obsessed with being a lady; instead she'd been giving her advice. Grandma Dia always told her to go out with at least a pickaxe and shovel. Grandma Dia always insisted she watch the time of day. *Grandma Dia always had faith in me.*

Grandma Dia believed she could handle anything. She believed that Alison shouldn't go adventuring, but never told her she was unable to do so. Grandma Dia hid her advice in a lot of stern reprimands; Alison hadn't been listening closely. "Why didn't you just tell me?" she whispered aloud, a tear dripping down her face.

If Boots had been there, they would have found Nicholas, convinced Freya to leave the Nether, and been home by dinnertime.

After pacing the room, taking deep breaths, Alison felt she had control again. She went to the crafting table and got to work.

These skeletons were not the ones that Bunny Biter had led away. Max could tell Freya was getting worried, since they had yet to find the wolf, but the skeletons they approached were acting oddly all the same.

They neared the mobs cautiously, weapons ready, and found the skeletons weren't chasing something, but milling about in a confused manner, waving their swords and bows around.

"What are they doing?" Max whispered, edging closer. He gripped his sword tighter, convinced this had to be a trick.

"Never mind that; what are they carrying?" Freya asked.

These skeletons looked like skeletons usually did, either in an occasional piece of armor or wearing nothing but bones—but some carried colorful banners instead of weapons.

The skeleton closest to them was carrying a garish pink banner with the image of a blue horse on the front. Max recognized it with a shock: Alison's mother had made it.

Alison's mother had loved to knit with the brightly colored wool her sheep produced, and she gave the banners out on holidays. Max owned two himself, but he had packed them away, as he didn't want to upset Alison.

But now he felt his own grief well up in his throat as he realized the blue horse banner had been a gift from Alison's mother to his own Uncle Nicholas.

"The banner. It was Nicholas's. Alison's mom made it," he said to Freya in a strangled voice.

"What is he doing to those skeletons?" Freya asked, scrunching up her nose. "Has the Nether made him lose his mind?"

"What if that skeleton *is* Nicholas?" Max said.

She shook her head. "Nah. That's not the way it works. Skeletons are not some silly reanimation of a dead person. They are monsters that spawn in dark places. That's just science, Max." She looked at Max with something akin to intellectual pity, like she was sorry for him because he fell asleep in class too often.

"Besides," she continued. "Your uncle is behind this, for sure. Check out its helmet."

Max had been so distracted by the colorful banner that he hadn't noticed the reason the skeleton had been staggering around: it wore a helmet backward on its head. It swung its banner through the air like a sword, flailing about, clearly unable to see anything.

It pulled at the helmet with its free hand, but the thing wouldn't budge. Freya laughed. "That's your uncle's enchanting, right there. I don't know why he's got them carrying banners. But Nicholas is around here somewhere."

Max's grief evaporated into something like hope as he realized she was right. With a quick slice of his sword, he took down the skeleton; it fell to the ground and disappeared, leaving its stone sword, the cursed helmet, and the banner behind.

Max picked up the banner and stowed it; he left the other stuff on the ground.

There were more skeletons, all wearing cursed armor that hindered them more than helped. Max and Freya found it easy to cut through them, heading in the direction the mobs were coming from.

Nicholas had to be sending these skeletons out; the only question was, why?

If the eyes of ender were in her pack, that meant they couldn't look at her, right?

Alison patted the pack nervously, trying not to think of those eyes flicking around in the darkness. They were too valuable to leave behind, but they sure were creepy.

She continued to inventory the supplies, stowing away water, obsidian, and stacks of food to keep the weird eyes company.

She needed to be prepared for anything. Boots would have told her a lady was always prepared, even if what it took to get prepared was unladylike.

Boots was unconcerned with paradox.

CHAPTER 23

NEW USES FOR CURSED ARMOR

<u>I am out of supplies.</u> I think about the items I have left behind me in various domiciles in the Nether, and I regret leaving so much behind. But a person can carry only so much, both physically and emotionally.

I fear I am at my end, now. If my final journals are found, please tell my family that I am sorry for the mistakes I've made. And tell the girl Freya I regret not taking her up on her hospitality. And tell Boots she was right. About most things, anyway.

How I ended up in this one room, surrounded by mobs, is embarrassing to say the least, but if I'm found this way, there will be questions. I have discovered a fortress I would like to inhabit but I needed some supplies, and found an ancient, crumbling structure nearby. I became greedy and wanted to search for specific items not found in my new home. I grew tired and built myself a single room to rest in safely. I built my room close to a crumbling wall, with hopes that the wall would add more protection, but it seems I didn't notice a nearby mob spawner. I took a quick rest, and when I peeked outside I was surrounded by enemies.

I'm trapped. I came here with a few weapons, considerable amounts of leather, a few crafting tables, and some food. But my weapons have all broken by now. They lie littered around me

I began crafting leather armor with the intent to curse them,
—cursing! How did I miss this in all my studies?

I thought I was placing an enchantment of binding on my items so that I would further bind an enchantment, and instead I was cursing them with the inability to remove the item until it broke. I've left cursed armor in my wake throughout the Nether until I realized what I was doing. Now I'm doing it to save my life.

I can place a cursed helmet backward on the skeleton's head, and it will wander away in confusion. I've tried to give them banners to carry, to perhaps alert someone to my presence, but I haven't seen another soul in some time. And there are always more skeletons.

I'm keeping them from attacking me, but I am nearly out of leather.

I ran out of food yesterday.

The mobs keep coming.

. . .

Bunny Biter was there, barking furiously at a skeleton carrying a blue banner, when Max and Freya found the dark corner where the monsters were coming from, nestled in an alley between a newer simple one-room building and a crumbling wall. The wolf had dropped (or eaten) the skeleton leg along the way, and looked to be searching for another snack. She'd dart in, nip at the skeleton's heels, and then dart out, barking. She seemed confused by the skeleton's inability to attack directly, and thought barking was the safest bet.

When her mistress called her, she perked her head up immediately and teleported to Freya's side. Freya took a moment to kneel and hug her wolf, whose tail was wagging furiously, and then she stood.

The blinded monsters milled about outside the small building, some looking in windows as if they didn't have a helmet stuck the wrong way on their heads, others wandering away in confusion. "I'm betting your uncle is inside there," Freya said, pointing.

"Do you think you and Bunny Biter can take care of these skeletons out here while I clear out the mobs by the path to the door?" Max asked.

Freya gave him a withering look. "Do you really need to ask?" She winked at him. "Bunny Biter, sic tibia!" she called to the wolf, who was immediately off again, aiming for the nearest skeleton's leg. Freya raised her bow and began loosing arrows one after the other.

Max took a moment to admire her, wondering how long he and Alison would have lasted in the Nether without their new friend. Then he ran in a wide arc around the little shelter, avoiding the mobs and looking for their source.

He saw immediately that the shack was built amid the ruins of a crumbling fortress. This one had to have been here much longer than the others he had noticed, as it had no roof, and more walls than not were skeletal representations of their old strength. But monsters could still spawn in this old fortress, and they were doing so with a vengeance.

His pack contained his good armor just in case he found a way to lose the cursed items, some food, a few minor pieces of loot picked up from the skeletons, and the diamond pickaxe Alison had made for him. He stashed his diamond sword and gripped the pickaxe. He had to clear out the monsters and get some torches on the wall to make the area safer. He just needed to trust that Freya and Bunny Biter would do their part of the job.

Max put down some blocks of netherrack and climbed to a ledge at the mouth of the alley, where he could see the entryway into the small building. From his vantage point, he saw with a pang of regret the vast expanse of the fortress. It must have been truly amazing when it was whole. Now it was just a dangerous ruin. He gave a thought as to what his mom would say if she were here, and he grinned sadly. He missed even her yelling at him.

He wished Alison could see him now—he was being careful! He crept a few blocks forward until he was looking down on the milling skeletons, thickest in the dark alley between the newer building and the crumbling fortress wall. A few options ran through his mind: he could try to build a walkway above the mobs and all the way over to the door; he could try to stick a few torches on the walls to drive them out of the alley; or he could fire down a few arrows from his hiding place and pick them off from there.

Each plan had its pros and cons, but before he could decide, one skeleton finally noticed him and shot an arrow in his direction.

Max abandoned his method of careful planning and jumped straight down into the fray of skeletons, whooping and swinging his sword with his right hand. With his left, he waved a torch around until he saw an opening and stuck it to the wall.

Bunny Biter snarled behind him, and he heard clacking as another skeleton went down. His diamond sword bit into skeleton after skeleton, severing skulls and whacking swords out of bony hands. He was in a brightly lit area now, and the skeletons were starting to run from the wolf.

Something punched him from behind and he stumbled forward in surprise, whirling to see a skeleton that had snuck up behind him. It waved its sword at him, and Max raised his own sword too slowly, his arm aching.

Behind the skeleton, the shelter wall crumbled as the tip of a pickaxe came through the loose stone. The skeleton's blank face disappeared behind a leather helmet. It staggered forward, suddenly unable to see. Max took the opportunity and gave a mighty swing of his sword, felling the skeleton.

"Max?" said a strangled voice from the darkness of the building's interior, but Max didn't waste time. He put up the remaining torches and made sure no more skeletons were coming from any dark corners. Then he turned, breathing hard, and grinned at the figure looking through the hole in the wall. "Hey, Uncle Nicholas. Ready to go home?"

Max was enveloped in a hug so tight he couldn't breathe, and he had a bizarre flashback to when he was drowning, but thankfully his uncle let him go. Nicholas pulled him through the hole he'd made in the wall and quickly patched it back up.

"Max! How— Why— When—" He was unable to get anything out. Max just grinned at him.

"Is there room for two more in there?" The door opened on the other side of the room, making them both jump. Freya and Bunny Biter came in.

"Freya?" Nicholas seemed even more baffled to see her. "What's going on here? How do you know each other?"

"First, are you okay? Injured or anything?" Max asked. His uncle looked like he could use a comb and a bath, but otherwise seemed whole and healthy.

"I'm fine, but—" He looked from Max to Freya, confusion and delight warring on his face.

Max began to give him an account of everything that had happened, starting with the "drowning" and discovering Nicholas's cabin. "And then Alison and I went back home and—"

"Wait," Nicholas said, "Alison is living with you?"

"Oh, yeah, I forgot that part," Max said, glad that Alison wasn't there to see him squirm over the fact that he'd forgotten about her family. "Soon after you, uh, left, her house was destroyed by a creeper. She's the only one left."

Nicholas looked like he had been struck in the chest. He staggered backward, stunned, and leaned against the wall. Max remembered that he and Alison's grandma had once been friends.

"Everyone?" Nicholas asked. "Even Dia?"

"They didn't find anyone after the explosion except Alison," Max said softly. "So Mom invited her to move in with us."

Nicholas rubbed his face and sighed, looking very sad, and then returned from whatever nostalgia he had been visiting. "Go on," he finally said.

Max told the story of the second creeper attack, the chicken jockey attack, Freya's rescue, and how they had hunted for him.

"Hey, I have a question. Why did you put a bunch of mobs in a glass box?" Freya asked him.

"Seemed like a good idea at the time," Nicholas said. "I built three sides, then lured them over there. Inside is a trapdoor that I escaped through. It kept me busy making the island safe, but then the mobs would still spawn. It was a waste of time."

Max finished the tale of their adventures with leaving Alison at the fortress and coming to find him. "And now we can take you back and figure out a way to get a portal home!"

Nicholas sobered up. "I don't know, your mom made it pretty clear she didn't want me back."

"Then move to another house, one that isn't in the village," Freya said. "There are a lot of places that aren't the Nether, you know. You don't have to live in this desolate place."

Max cocked an eyebrow at her. "I thought *you* had chosen to live in this desolate place?"

Freya grinned and shrugged. "Alison reminded me that I missed the color green."

Both enchanters had wanted to explore the crumbled fortress because of the treasures that could be inside, but Freya reminded them that Alison was alone and waiting for them.

On the way back, Max asked Nicholas why he was so upset about Alison's family. "I mean, I was sad too, but you took it personally."

Nicholas sighed. "It was a long time ago. She never wanted us to tell you. Many years ago, Alison's Grandma Dia, her Grandpa Robert, and I were close friends. Robert had no taste for adventuring, though; he wanted to stay home and keep his animals safe. Dia had a strong curiosity but also an aversion to danger, so she came with me but complained the whole time." He smiled fondly at the memory. "She didn't want to admit she enjoyed it. But I would craft items and make our shelters, and she would enchant the items and do whatever alchemy we needed. She hated visiting the Nether, though, but went because she said she had to keep me out of trouble."

Max listened, his mouth hanging open. He was dimly aware of Freya scanning their surroundings for monsters as he stared at his uncle. "Are you serious?"

He nodded sadly. "I called her 'Boots' because that's what her last name meant. We stopped adventuring when she started a family, and she became very maternal, not wanting any of her kids to explore the same places she had. One more time, when her children were young, she and I went to the Nether. Her leg was badly injured in a wither skeleton attack, and I got her back home. She made a full recovery, but from then on she would have nothing to do with the Nether, and made me and Alison's grandfather swear never to tell the families what we had been up to in our youth."

He grinned down at Max. "Looks like it didn't matter anyway, since you and Alison are doing exactly what we had done."

Max winced. "So that's why Grandma Dia limped?"

Nicholas shook his head. "That was just age catching up with her. I told her that was the case, but she didn't like that very much and decided to blame me, even though I was the one who fought the skeleton off her. Still, she wouldn't have been in the Nether if it weren't for me. If she knew you two were here right now, she would be an avenging angel, limp or no limp, coming to find you two."

Max laughed, picturing Dia swooping in to save—and scold—them, then grimaced. "You and I might be too similar, actually." He told Nicholas the story of the cursed armor, both the armor he himself had cursed, and the faulty armor he had looted from Nicholas's house.

Nicholas grasped his shoulders. "Oh, my boy, you were not to follow in my footsteps! My footsteps are weighed down by cursed boots and fermented spider eyes!" His eyebrows came together, making his face look like a thundercloud, reminding Max forcefully of his mother. They looked very much alike right then. Then Nicholas relaxed and was himself again. "I'm so grateful you're alive. Just promise me you're learning from my mistakes."

Max thought about the failed experiments. "I'm learning from yours and mine, yeah."

"As long as you're learning. And alive."

"But my enchantments work! Sometimes," Max added. "And I'm learning more and more."

"That is more than I can say, sadly. Right now, the only thing I've achieved is a new use for cursed armor. I'm amazed you've managed to make some items that were successfully enchanted." Nicholas inspected Freya's boots. "Did you enchant these?"

"Oh yeah, among a bunch of failures."

"Well, that's how you learn!" Nicholas said, delighted. "You learn all the ways to not do something, and then you find the way to do it. I've found many, many ways *not* to enchant armor. I just recently learned that step one is not to curse the armor with binding. I will eventually figure out step two."

"Until then you have a unique business model," Freya suggested. *"Just jam one of Nicholas's Cursed Caps on the heads of any mob following you and they will be unable to get it off, leaving you and your family safe and secure!"*

Nicholas thought for a moment. "That might work, actually."

Max swallowed, nervous all of a sudden. "Then does that mean you're coming home with us?"

His uncle's face darkened again. "The Overworld doesn't have Dia in it. We were good friends."

"But it does have Mom. And me, and Alison," Max said, hurt.

Nicholas smiled and hugged Max. "True. Let's get to safety and we can talk more."

CHAPTER 24

ALISON IS BOOTS ALL OVER AGAIN

Alison didn't know what to expect when they brought Nicholas back, but when he gave her a look that was nothing but compassion, and she realized he was missing her grandma as much as she was, she burst into tears. Nicholas opened his arms and she ran in for a hug.

"I keep feeling like I could have stopped it," she whispered.

"And I keep feeling like I could have helped if I hadn't run away here," he said. "But there's probably nothing we could have done, in all honesty, Alison. I'm so sorry. I never got to tell your Grandma that she was right about almost everything. I still can't believe something as mundane as a creeper took out that old adventurer."

He held her at arm's length. "But you know what she would say to us right now, don't you?"

Alison sniffled. "Probably something like, *A lady never cries at an inopportune moment. Now wipe those tears off your face. You can cry when you're home safe.*"

Nicholas smiled. "Exactly."

"So, wait, you knew about your grandparents and my uncle?" Max asked as he watched them.

"I only just figured it out after you left," she said, holding up the book she'd been reading. "I found her journal."

Nicholas smiled as he looked at the well-preserved book, gently taking it from Alison and turning it over in his hands. "She'd want you to keep this safe," he said after a moment, handing it back to her. He gently patted her on the shoulder, then turned to Max. "We need to get you kids safely home. What do you have ready to go?"

Max looked sheepish for a moment before explaining that they'd used most of their supplies to find him. Before Uncle Nicholas could say anything, Freya began listing what they'd need and giving jobs to everyone. Alison shared a grin with Max behind Freya's back before she turned to her assignment: inventory current supplies in the various chests. She reached into her pack and pulled out a list she'd already made, but everyone had already started busily working on their own jobs. Bunny Biter sat at Freya's feet as she brewed potions in the corner, Max prepared food, and Uncle Nicholas unpacked the supplies he'd brought as he patiently answered the questions Max peppered him with as he worked.

Alison watched as Nicholas shelved the enchanting books he'd brought with him. He did it with the care of a father putting a baby to bed. She was nervous; knowing what she did about this man now, and the kindness he'd shown her, she didn't want to be a thief, but she had also seen the wreckage his enchanting had caused. She didn't want to see him enchant something that put them all in danger, even if he did it by accident. Her mind wandered back to all of the havoc he had inadvertently caused with fermented spider eyes, and she shivered. Yes, she was impressed with Nicholas's innovation with the cursed armor, but he still made her nervous.

And even though the stories Nicholas was telling them about his adventures with Grandma Dia were very entertaining, she had to admit that one common thread connected them all. Grandma Dia hadn't trusted Nicholas to make good decisions on his own. Not when they were younger, and not when they were older.

Then again, no one had expected Alison to make her own decisions either. And she was actually careful.

She owed him the benefit of the doubt, hoping he had learned from all the disasters. She certainly had. She walked over to one of the chests, opened it, and replaced the eyes of ender that she had originally planned to hide from him. They belonged to Nicholas. Boots was no longer around to guide him, but Alison hoped he would make good decisions anyway.

Finally the group relaxed on the floor, all of them free from the confining armor—except Max—with spare banners beneath them to make it more comfortable.

"You know I ran before they found you," he said sadly. "I was so ashamed, I couldn't look Rose in the face. I had gone to the Nether several times long ago, but each time was with Boots. I had ventured there a few times more recently by myself, and was more and more interested in taking you there. Once you were gone I lost my head a bit, enchanted a bunch of things, and then I just ran through the portal. But now you've found me and we can go home." He took a drink from his canteen. "I think I'm ready."

Alison was about to interrupt, but Max perked up and said, "You're coming with us?"

Uncle Nicholas nodded. "You need someone to escort you

there, and I owe you some actual guardianship rather than just being a bad example. And I've already failed you so many times. Even when I wasn't around," he said, gesturing to Max's still-equipped armor. "It's what Boots would expect from me."

Alison chuckled. "She would not! She would say you were a fool for coming back here and likely getting yourself into your own mess."

Nicholas held up a finger. "Ah, but what would she say once she was done yelling at me? *Just get those kids out safely so I can—*"

"*—be angry in the privacy of my own home!*" Alison finished, and they both laughed. "I guess you're right." She cleared her throat and grew serious. "But the portal is gone. We have no idea where it is. We got chased, and lost, and now can't even begin to backtrack. What do you suggest we do?"

Nicholas scratched at his scraggly beard. "What would Boots do?"

"After she was done yelling, she would take inventory, get the bare minimum of obsidian, or—" Alison thought hard, the answer right at the tip of her tongue.

"Or *make* it," Max said. "We're surrounded by lava. All we need is a source for lava and a diamond pickaxe."

"We've got the pickaxe," Freya said. "And we are definitely not short on lava. We just need to find the source of one of these lakes."

"That won't be hard." Nicholas got to his feet, looking tired but determined. "Who wants to go home?"

CHAPTER 25

ALISON AND MAX WISH
THEY RAN TRACK IN SCHOOL

As they checked their equipment and readied themselves, Alison thought back to the stories Grandma Dia had told her. She wondered how many of the wild *and then my sheep got lost and I had to go far away to find them* stories that Alison had heard had been cleverly disguised Nether stories. Tears pricked her eyes again as she wished her grandma was still around.

"Where are we going to build this?" Max asked. "Right outside?"

"We build it wherever we can find the lava source," Nicholas said. "We're not hauling the obsidian back here. No point. We'll just hope we avoid any attacks along the way."

Freya shook her head sharply, testing the string on her bow. "You don't avoid attacks in the Nether. You fight them, delay them, or hide until you starve. I usually choose to fight."

Alison handed Freya the last bow. "I will be so glad to get home." She wondered how life would be different now, with Nicholas back, trying to reconcile with Max's family, and Max working to learn more enchanting with his uncle. She felt an unexpected double-edged pang of jealousy, since Nicholas returning would give Max another adventuring partner, and Max would have gotten his wish and had his family member returned, while she was still alone.

She shook her head. She wasn't going to begrudge Max his beloved uncle. And besides, she would have to help Freya get acclimated to wherever she wanted to settle.

"When we get back to the Overworld, what are you going to do?" Alison asked Freya, who sat with her pack on the floor against the wall, petting Bunny Biter.

"What do you mean?"

"You don't have a family, or a home, do you? Did you have a plan?" Alison paused, and when Freya didn't answer, she said, "You could come live with me. I don't have much of a place: my house needs rebuilding, but I could use the company. Max will be busy with Nicholas for a while, I expect. I think his family should figure out how they work together on their own. They have some fences to mend."

Freya was still silent. Alison raised her head to see what was wrong. Freya had buried her face into Bunny Biter's fur, and the wolf made a low whine in her throat.

"Freya?"

"I've been worried about returning to the Overworld. Maybe I'll just stay here," Freya said.

"But there's no reason—"

"Yes, there is. If I am here then I'm always busy fighting for my life and I don't have to face the fact that I'm alone. When I don't have constant mob attacks to worry about, then I have to worry about my reality. My family is gone."

Pity and an all too familiar ache rose in Alison's chest, and she put a hand on her friend's arm. "I know what you mean. But you're not alone anymore. You have us," she said.

Freya lifted her face from the fur. She looked vulnerable and very sad, and Alison realized just how alone Freya had been.

Freya took a deep breath, then nodded. "All right. I'll live with you. You'll need someone to protect you from those creepers. Seems your area is infested with them."

There's the old Freya. Alison grinned wider and started to figure out what she could carry in her nearly full pack. There were a lot of things to take back home.

She glanced across the room to Max and Nicholas. They were poring over books and speaking in low voices with a bow between them. Alison checked her equipment to make sure they weren't enchanting *her* bow—good, it was in her pack already.

The enchanting table hissed, and Nicholas groaned. "Do not pick that up," he commanded, and swept the bow off the table using a stick.

Alison sighed and hoped they would make it home in the first place.

"I don't want you fighting," Nicholas said, flipping through an enchanting book.

"What? I've been doing fine so far!" Max protested. His uncle had been in an increasingly parental mood since they had reunited. Max had once wondered how his uncle and his mom could be siblings, but now he saw it.

"Yes, and you've been hit several times," Nicholas said, pausing to look up and point to the nicks and scorch marks on Max's armor that showed his past few days' adventures. "You will wear that armor until the last hit, when it will fail, and then it will disintegrate. After that, what are you going to do? Ask the mobs to wait a moment while you run out of the battle to put on more armor?"

Max shrugged. That was exactly what he had planned. He could change armor and weapons pretty quickly.

"We will need to make it through this, and then we can figure out a way to carefully damage the armor to get it off you safely," Nicholas said. "Until then, you need to stay out of the line of fire."

"Freya just wanted to dangle me in lava to burn it off," Max said bitterly, but thinking that it might be a better choice than just sitting around waiting for it to rot off.

"That is about as good an idea as sending you into battle with leather armor," Nicholas said.

"Then what am I supposed to do? Just wear this for the rest of my life?" Max said, exasperated.

"No, when we get back home we can push you down several times until the armor just pops off," Nicholas said.

Max stared at him. "I can't tell if you're kidding."

The mood was not as upbeat as they'd have liked when they left the fortress, weighed down by considerable supplies and extra equipment. Max was highly distracting, running purposefully into the walls and nearly pitching himself down stairs before Alison grabbed his arm.

"I regret suggesting this," Nicholas said, closing his eyes as Max fell flat on his face and got back to his feet. Max ran ahead, followed by Nicholas and Alison, with Freya bringing up the rear.

"It could work," Alison said doubtfully. "But what happens if only part of the equipment pops off?"

"Exactly," Nicholas said.

Alison sighed. "We're in danger, and you suggested he run into walls until the armor falls off?"

"To be fair, I suggested he do it when we get home."

"We should stop him," Alison said. "We don't want him charging at more magma cubes."

Speaking of magma cubes, Nicholas caught sight of about four of them far to the left, leaping up and down a cliff as if gravity didn't apply to them. The group elected to skirt around them widely to avoid catching their attention. Alison was interested in trying her pit-trap idea again, if she were to encounter more magma cubes, but they all agreed that not engaging was the best plan.

"We avoided *that* fight," Alison told Freya as they left the danger behind them.

"Sure, until the next time," Freya said, aiming her bow at a zombie pigman wandering around nearby. It ignored them, and she slowly relaxed.

"So, about that wither skeleton prison," Freya said, and Nicholas turned to her as Max fell in at his uncle's side.

"It was highly complex and probably too much effort if the pigmen could get out like that," he said. "But when they started spawning in my storage room, I built a tunnel to the mushroom farm. They'd follow the tunnel and get trapped in the prison."

"Why didn't you just take down the mobs?" Max said, panting slightly.

His uncle looked at him like the answer was obvious. "Because I'm a builder, and it's easier for me to build a tunnel and a trapdoor than fight a roomful of wither skeletons."

"But that doesn't make sense," Max said. "You're still dealing with monsters in your storage room before they decide to wander down the tunnel, and you get more and more monsters; but killing them where they come from means only fighting once."

"Not much down here makes sense," Nicholas said.

Max's armor was starting to chafe.

Actually, it had started to chafe hours before. Right now, it was downright painful. And his body was bruised from falling down so much. It sounded like good logic, getting rid of the armor before a fight, but now he was sore and it showed no sign of weakening. His uncle wouldn't let him do much more than that; there was too much danger. If the armor absorbed just a little bit of a blow before it fell off, his body would take the rest of the attack's damage. And that didn't sound like fun at all.

He shifted, trying to readjust the cursed pieces, and gritted his teeth. If he complained about it, they'd all say that he'd brought it on himself. Which he had done, but that was beside the point.

He wasn't sure *what* the point was, anymore. He had his uncle back; he just wanted to get home. The annoying armor situation was starting to get to him, and the heat wasn't making his frustration any easier to bear. A bead of sweat rolled down his forehead and into his eye. He gave his eyes an irritated rub, and when he looked back up, he saw a magma cube hopping toward him from the top of a hill.

Max and Uncle Nicholas ran up the hill, hitting the occasional magma cube that hopped into their path. Uncle Nicholas had said that if you struck them as they were about to land on you, then you could bat them away, damaging them in the process. He missed Bone Bane's enchantment and had to use sheer force to make the cubes sail into the distance, but it was a good way to vent his frustration. Whacking the things away made fights much easier, as long as they were alert.

Freya and Alison took care of any blazes that threatened them from afar, warning Max and Nicholas when incoming fire got too close. Bunny Biter chased any encroaching mobs away.

This whole "adventuring in the Nether" thing was getting easy! All they had needed was a group of four, and some solid weapons. At the top of the hill, Nicholas pointed. "There."

They'd seen the glow of the lava from behind the hill, but now it was a truly impressive landscape. The canyon ended in a sunken lava pool, with netherrack all around, fire geysers erupting nearby, and lava falls spewing from a wall above the pool. When a fire geyser erupted right in front of the pool, Max and Alison shouted in alarm, both pointing: an unfinished portal already stood there, one full corner created. Max wondered who had abandoned the project, or what terrible person had attacked the frame with a diamond pickaxe. Regardless, it was more of a portal than they'd had before.

"I didn't think we'd make it!" Alison said, relief and happiness in her voice.

"And it's already started for us!" Freya said, noticing the obsidian too.

"The only thing is, what happened to the person who started to build that in the first place?" Alison asked.

"Maybe they changed their minds?" Max said, and Alison glared at him.

"I think we have a good idea of what happened," Nicholas said quietly, pointing to a pack and a diamond pickaxe lying next to the unfinished portal.

"So we'll be on the lookout," Freya said, patting her wolf. "No big deal."

"A little late for that," Nicholas said, "and I think we should run to get out of here as soon as possible." He was facing behind them instead of at the portal ahead, and before they could ask why, he turned and extended his arms, shepherding them all down the hill.

Behind them, Max could hear a chilling scream. He took a chance and glanced backward, seeing a floating white body crest the hill, heading right for them.

"There's no cover, where are we going?" Freya yelled.

"Right now I'd rather be close to the portal than far from it!" Max said.

"Come on, kids, stop arguing and run!" Nicholas called.

"I read what Grandma Dia wrote," Alison said, running beside Nicholas. "This is a ghost, isn't it?" Its scream was terrifying, sounding like wailing babies who were scratching their nails down an ice block. While a ghost was chasing them.

A *whoosh* sounded, and Alison cried, "Duck!" They all crouched lower, still trying to run. The fireball heated Alison's exposed neck, but it missed them.

Their luck turned immediately when the fireball kept sailing ahead, straight for the portal.

"No!" Max shouted, but it clipped the portal on the side and bounced away to sail across the lava. "I forgot obsidian was that strong," Max said.

Alison felt fear claw at her throat, the sheer terror of the ghast reminding her of creepers. "How are we going to fight and build at the same time?" she asked, slowing.

Max ran back and grabbed her hand. "It's not a problem. We can split up. We're a good team. Some can build, some can fight. We have lava, we have water, we have a pickaxe, we have people who can build. But first we have to stay alive; then we have to finish building it. Then we can get out of here," he said, and pulled her into a run.

They ended up right on the edge of the lava pool next to the portal. Nicholas stood with his diamond sword raised, with Alison and her bow and Max and his new, unenchanted sword behind him. Freya climbed to the top of a small hill to the left and started loosing arrows at the ghast.

It shot another fireball, making them all duck. It sailed straight through the portal's frame.

"If it was complete, we could go through it right now!" Max shouted.

"Yeah, and—" Alison said, but then interrupted herself. "Duck!"

They had taken their eyes off the ghast while looking at the portal, and now narrowly avoided being hit by another fireball.

"We have to take care of that ghast," Freya said grimly, shooting more arrows. It was getting closer now, but at least that made it a bigger target. She hit true a few times, and the ghast deflated and went down in a pile of white flailing tentacles, and then it was no more. Max leaped into the air, pumping his fist and shouting, "Yeah!" Freya grinned at him, before turning to Alison.

"Alison, go loot the tears," Freya said. "Before Bunny Biter eats them."

Alison took a furtive look around, and ran out to find anything the ghast may have dropped.

"Is everybody all right?" Nicholas asked, looking them all over anxiously.

"Yeah," Max said, panting. "Now what do we do about the portal?"

Nicholas pointed to a crack in the wall from where the lava streamed. "We need to get up there and get some water into that lava. Then mine it."

"Oh, is that all," Alison said, handing Freya the white tears that had hovered over the ghast's body.

"I'm on it, no problem," Max said, building steps to get to the hole in the cliff.

"Hey, everybody," Freya said, her voice way too calm for Alison's comfort. "It's not over."

Across the Nether landscape, they heard the screams of more approaching ghasts.

CHAPTER 26

NICHOLAS'S TERRIBLE ARMOR IS USEFUL

Nicholas started to build a wall for them to hide behind so they could think of how to deal with the numerous ghasts that had decided to join their party.

Alison put her hand on his shoulder. "Netherrack is about as soft as wood. Do you really think this will stop a fireball?"

"Boots said they're lazy. If they can't see us, we're safer than if they can!" he countered, and got to work. Freya jumped from her perch and joined them. Once they had a three-by-three wall, Nicholas pushed the group out of the way of one of the fireballs that came sailing toward them and they huddled behind the barrier. They took a moment to breathe.

The ghasts still screamed, but they had stopped their assault. Above them, Max had built his own two-by-two shield as he poured his water onto the lava, wincing at the steam that came out. He began hacking at the resulting black block.

"Now what do we do?" Alison asked.

"Our options are," Nicholas said, crouching down, ". . . nothing. I have no ideas. Fight until Max gets what we need, I guess." He looked at the portal and made a quick calculation. "Max, we need five more blocks!" he called up to his nephew.

"Or fight until we beat them," Freya said, standing up and shooting another arrow before she crouched back down. "Do you always give up this easily?"

"Leave it alone," Nicholas said. "Boots—"

"—isn't here," Alison said gently. "But we are. We're trying to get you home but we need your help."

A fireball crashed into the hill beside them, showering them with soul sand and embers. Max shouted when his leather armor caught fire, and Nicholas tossed him a canteen to put himself out.

"He's got two blocks," Alison said, retrieving them as Max dropped them. "But we're going to fight. They're pretty vulnerable to arrows. Freya and I will shoot at them, and Nicholas, those fireballs are pretty solid. If you use your sword, you might be able to whack the fireballs back at them. Max needs to build—"

"Hey, I can fight if someone else does this! It's not like it's enchanting or anything!" Max said indignantly.

"You stay back here," she repeated, her voice hard. "Yes, because we want to keep you safe, but also because you need to finish building the portal. Sometimes we have to help out how we best can, not how we want to."

"You should write a book," he grumbled. "You sound very inspirational. Also really annoying."

"That's because I'm right," Alison said, pulling out her bow and arrows. "Oh, and here," she added, tossing her pack up to him.

.   .   .

Max chipped away at the obsidian, tongue held in his teeth, wanting to argue that he could take on any screaming white clouds that spit fireballs. But he peeked inside Alison's pack and saw, among other things, two bookcases, an enchanting table, and three more canteens of water. She had packed everything she thought they would need.

"You're trusting me with this?" he yelled to her as she took a high spot beside Freya.

"I gave it to you, didn't I?" she asked. "Get us home."

Max took a long look at the enchanting table, and thought about his diamond sword, and his uncle's sword, and how great it would be if they were enchanted.

He shook his head, hefted his pickaxe, and went back to excavating obsidian blocks. He tried to concentrate as he worked, but his friends and his uncle weren't making it easy with their struggles.

Freya and Alison were doing well from their perch. Looking like she had learned something from their bridge adventure, Freya had built a climbing staircase out of netherrack and ascended from the hill to the top of the portal itself, to get a better shot. Unfortunately, that made them bigger targets, and right after they took one ghast down, another came straight at them with a fireball. Freya dodged, but Alison took it full-force and flew backward, flaming, into the lava. Max yelled and ran to the edge of the pool, but there was nothing he could do without burning himself and his horrible armor.

He watched, shocked, as her golden helmet appeared and she surfaced, then climbed out. She looked slightly burned, but all right overall.

"What did you—"

"I had another potion of fire protection," she said. "Not sure how much longer I have, but at least it saved me that time." She took a deep, shaking breath and grinned. "I don't think I ever want to go near lava again." She readied her bow and ran back to help Freya.

Uncle Nicholas was doing a pretty good job of whacking the fireballs away from the girls and Max, so Max was finally able to mine the final obsidian block they needed. He jumped down to the unfinished portal frame and put the first block into place. Before he could put the second one in, though, he heard Uncle Nicholas yell as he missed one of the fireballs. Max had to leap out of the way to avoid being roasted.

Another ghast scream sounded, and another enemy fell; the fighting team didn't let up. Max looked up from where he'd landed and was dismayed; the ground was littered with ghast tears, but there were still an endless number of ghasts filling the air with fireballs. Every once in a while, someone would get hit and catch fire, but they seemed to be doing all right.

Every few hours during his time in the Nether, it seemed Max had to adjust what "all right" meant. Seeing his best friend on fire, put herself out, and then keep shooting arrows at screaming, fire-belching clouds wouldn't have been "all right" even yesterday. Max shook his head and quickly slapped a few more blocks into place.

Only one more left!

A trio of fireballs hit Freya, and she fell back off the portal, landing hard inches from the lava. Max ran over and quickly poured a canteen of water on her and put the fire out, but she looked in bad shape. Her potion must have worn off.

"Max, finish the portal!" Alison shouted, and ran to Freya with a healing potion. Nicholas took up the post to protect them while Alison did her field medicine, but several ghasts shot at once. Nicholas tried to dodge, but tripped over the girls and went into the lava.

Max started toward him, and then glanced back at the portal, which needed one more block. "Alison, can you get him out?" he yelled, and Alison was on it, wincing as her own armor caught fire when she reached into the lava.

Covered in burns, Nicholas groaned as Alison pulled him out. Max was the only healthy one among them, and all that protected him was crappy, cursed leather armor.

The ghasts had closed in and started to surround the unfinished portal. He remembered something he had heard from Freya, and stood up. "Get everyone over to the portal, behind the shield!" he yelled to Alison, who weakly shouted back that she would.

Max sprinted toward the portal, slapping the final block into place as he passed it. He continued to run, heading straight out onto the battlefield as he yelled, jumping up and down. "Hey! You ugly fog monsters! I hear you're stupid enough to kill yourselves, is that true?"

The ghasts circled him on every side. Two of them fired at that moment, three fireballs each, and he threw himself to the ground. One of them passed too close over him, and he felt the diamond helm on his head crack slightly. His ear got singed as the fireball flew over him. He leaped back onto his feet. He was still surrounded.

That hadn't worked. He grimaced. He edged back a little to see if he could get the angle right, and taunted them again.

"I heard a bunch of creepers talking yesterday and they said you guys were complete wimps. They wanted to have a creeper–ghast brawl, in fact! I think they're going to jump you at the next full moon."

He wasn't sure if they knew what a moon was, but he had successfully taunted them, and they screamed again and launched more fire across the circle, all aiming for him.

He leaped to the side and rolled, none of the projectiles hitting him this time, and one ghast screamed as it took an ally's fireball in the face and deflated.

The others screamed as if Max had been the one to destroy the ghast, and they fired again. There were five left, and he had no more chances to taunt them; they were well and truly bent on his destruction. The fireballs soared toward him from all sides, cutting across the circle, and another ghast fell. He would have felt triumphant, but at the same time one of the fireballs bounced in front of him and burned away what was left of his helmet.

"Hey, I'm free!" he said, as the hated thing fell off him. But then he realized his head was unprotected, and there were four ghasts left.

He heard a thrum, and chanced a look behind him. One of the ghasts had lit the portal, and it shimmered with a purple glow. "Get through the portal now!" he yelled at his friends.

He heard the ghasts scream around him, and saw two more fall to their own friendly fire. With a *whoosh*, another fireball sailed toward the portal and hit it, putting out the glowing purple fire. Max let out a growl of frustration and turned back toward the remaining enemies while his friends ducked back behind his shield by the portal.

There were only two left. He could take two, right? Then he remembered he had Alison's pack, not his own, and there were no weapons here.

Another scream sounded in the distance. *More?*

This trip was a disaster, he thought, but then remembered that he had done what he set out to do: rescue Nicholas. He never promised it would be a clean and efficient job. Or a job where he would emerge uninjured and not saddled with cursed armor.

The armor. Right.

Max made his decision, and then a lot of things happened at once. He jumped up and ran toward the portal. Nicholas was crawling toward it, but Max didn't see Alison or Freya. Then Alison, looking ashy and determined, stepped out from behind the shield with her bow. She aimed above his head and shot her arrow. The ghast behind Max screamed. She shot again, and again, until it deflated.

There's only one left. And the one that was left fired its next attack right at Max as he turned to face it.

Max stood in front of the newly constructed portal and took the full force of the fireball blast. He felt his armor ignite, and the impact threw him backward into the portal. His burning outfit activated it, and he was pulled through.

His last thought before he passed out was, *I hope this gets that armor off, at least.*

CHAPTER 27

GHAST TEARS ARE NOT WOLF TREATS

Alison saw what Max was doing, and only hoped he could survive it, since she knew she couldn't stop him in time. He taunted the ghast into attacking him, the portal activated, and her friend was gone.

Alison ran up to Freya and shook her shoulder, hoping the healing potion had worked enough. Freya opened her eyes.

"The portal's working. You need to get Nicholas through," Alison said simply, and Freya nodded once and sat up. Alison ran back and shot more arrows at the remaining ghast, trying to get it to target her and not put out their precious portal.

A fireball passed too close to her, burning her shoulder. Her armor had taken a lot of damage at this point, and she didn't know how much longer it could last. She toppled backward with the impact, letting go one more arrow as she fell. She was sure it would sail wide, but as she landed painfully, she saw it go straight into the gassy bag that was the ghast's body, and the thing screamed once and was gone.

Alison lay panting for a moment, but realized that they weren't free yet. She still had to get Freya and Nicholas through the portal and then see if Max was all right.

She got up and ran to the portal where Freya stood, propping Nicholas on her shoulder, looking around.

"Bunny Biter. I can't find her!" she said.

Alison wanted to tell her she would find the wolf herself, and Freya should get Nicholas through the portal, but knew that Bunny Biter would only come to Freya. She took Nicholas's arm and nodded back to the field. "Go find her. But don't take too long. We'll wait for you on the other side."

Freya hugged her briefly, and Alison winced at the pressure on her burned and bruised body, but returned the hug tightly. Freya turned and ran off, and Alison pulled the nearly unconscious enchanter through the portal.

After every single thing he had been through, Max turned out to almost die by drowning after all.

He came to under cold water, his lungs burning, but he was grateful that nothing else was on fire. He swam to the surface and struggled toward land, finally collapsing onto warm sand, gasping. Burns covered his body and he was pretty sure his hair was gone. He could do nothing but lie there, coughing water out of his lungs, and being very aware of the sun in the bright sky overhead.

After he could breathe comfortably again, he realized the ghast had done him a favor by blowing the cursed armor off his body. He was finally free of the accursed pieces, and wore only his regular clothes, burned in several places as they were. He would have laughed in relief, but knowing the others were still in the

Nether was worrying. He didn't know if he should go back through or not. He had no armor, no weapons, nothing with which to help. But going back would answer the questions plaguing him. Had they made it past that last ghast? Could they move Nicholas?

He finally realized he should at least take in his surroundings. He painfully got to his feet and looked around. He had landed near the shoreline of a large body of water—so large that he couldn't see anything on the other side. The portal hung over the water, and he realized the others would also have a shock coming home. It also made the problem of going back to help them much harder, but he could build a platform to the portal. It would keep his mind off things.

Despite the cold water, it was very warm here, and the trees looked unfamiliar. He took down a few with some painful punches, and built a quick platform in front of the portal. Just as he finished giving the platform a path to the shore, Alison and Nicholas collapsed through the portal onto the platform.

Max ran to their side and helped them sit up. Nicholas was badly burned. Alison was injured but conscious. She handed Max his bag and he went rooting through it for more healing potions. He found one and put it to his uncle's lips.

"Where's Freya?" he asked Alison.

"She wouldn't come. She went looking for Bunny Biter," Alison said, removing her armor with a sigh. "Things were quiet when we left, so she'll probably be okay." She winced, as if a thought had occurred to her. "Or she was looking for an excuse to stay in the Nether and not come back with us."

Max shook his head firmly. "No. That's just not her. We'll wait for her, and then if she's not back by tomorrow, we'll get some stuff crafted so we can go back and look for her."

"Back?" Alison asked.

"For Freya," he said.

She nodded. "For Freya."

Max handed over her pack, and she got some mushrooms out of it and ate them, sighing with relief as the food strengthened her. "We might want to let your mom know we're okay first, though."

"She'll never let me go back if we do that," he said, laughing.

"Do you know which way home is from here?" Alison asked. "Nothing looks familiar."

Nicholas sat up suddenly. "Where's Freya?" he demanded. He looked around. "Where are we?"

"She's still in the Nether, and we're home," Max said. He looked around at the unfamiliar landscape and then added, "Sort of."

"She's looking for her wolf. She said she would be right behind us. And I'm not sure"—Alison looked around—"how close this is to home."

Nicholas stood up. "This isn't home. There is no body of water this large near our village." He squinted in the afternoon light, looking toward the north. "That's desert up there."

"Desert—there's no desert near home!" Max said. "How did we travel so far? We didn't go that far in the Nether!"

"Distance is different there. I should have remembered," Nicholas said. "What is one block there is several blocks here. Or the other way around. I don't remember. Boots would know. Anyway, the maps don't coincide."

"Don't worry, I've written it down," Alison said, holding up her own notebook.

.   .   .

The argument ranged from how long to wait for Freya, to whether they should set out for home immediately, to the wisdom of trying to find a village where they could get a map to make sure they were going in the right direction. Alison finally said they needed to first build a small shelter for the night and then they could decide their next step tomorrow. She then got very excited when she realized they could easily make real beds in a real shelter. She went out looking for some sheep while Nicholas and Max built their lodging.

Suddenly the purple glow of the portal activating shimmered intensely and Freya stepped out, holding Bunny Biter in her arms. Everyone was relieved at seeing them both safe, and Alison ran over to hug Freya tightly.

"I'm so happy you're safe! We were getting so worried."

"Yeah, what took you so long?" Max teased, giving Bunny Biter a pat on her head as the wolf sniffed around their new shelter.

"*Some*one—" Freya said, glaring at Bunny Biter.

"Don't you mean some*wolf*?" Alison asked, grinning at her.

Freya laughed, then said, "Yeah, actually, somewolf decided that ghast drops would be tasty, since skeleton drops were tasty. It turns out that wolf stomach doesn't like ghast tears nearly as much as bones. She was behind a rock horking up everything she'd eaten in the past few days."

She tossed her pack down on the ground. "I looted what I could, if you're interested," she said. "Just keep it away from the wolf."

Alison snatched up the pack before Bunny Biter's questing nose could find the "treats" inside.

Freya glanced around, frowning. "You live here? Where's the village?"

"No, actually," Alison said. "We are going to need to find our way home. We didn't know distances were different in the Nether and here."

Nicholas sighed. "I thought my challenge in coming back to the Overworld was going to be making amends with my family, rebuilding a tree house, and relieving a brother-in-law from doing my job. It looks like we have to find home first."

"You're going to make up with Mom and Dad?" Max asked.

"I'm going to try," Nicholas said. "I need to make up for a lot of mistakes. And I need to find someone to train me in enchanting, if I'm going to keep doing it. No more self-teaching." He smiled at Alison. "I owe Boots that much."

"And rebuilding a tree house?" Alison said. "Do you mean mine?" She glanced over at Freya, then said, "I mean *ours*."

Freya grinned.

"It's the least I could do," he said, before walking over to Alison. "And I also wanted to give you this." Nicholas reached into his pack, rummaging around for a moment before pulling out a small, tattered journal. He hesitated before handing it to her. "You remind me of your Grandma Boots. You're strong enough to tell me when I'm making questionable decisions instead of just going along with it for fear of speaking up. I'm glad you're Max's friend. So . . . here."

"What is this?" Alison took the journal, flipping it open to the first page. She immediately recognized the neat, almost stern handwriting.

"It is the journal your Grandma Dia used to chronicle our very first adventure together. She was much bolder in those days, young and brash as we were, and I wanted to share that with you." He smiled at Alison as she stared fixedly at the writing. "You really are so much like her at that age. I hope you find wisdom in its pages. And you"—he turned toward Max—"I hope you also learn something from my past mistakes!"

"Like don't use fermented spider eyes?" Max asked.

Nicholas let out a booming laugh. "Among many other things, yes." He looked at the sky, where the sun was rapidly sliding toward the horizon. "I love enchanting, but I have to learn the right way. When we get back, I'm going to find someone to teach me. Would you like to join me?"

A large grin split Max's face. "Yeah! Of course!"

Nodding, Nicholas said, "Wonderful! We'll get started as soon as we get back. For now, I think it's best that we all head inside and get some rest. It's going to be a long journey home."

Loud snores resounded off the walls as Nicholas slept. The kids stood at the window of their shelter, watching the mobs wander outside. To Max's eyes, they seemed tame compared to the other creatures they'd fought.

"I did miss green," Freya said. "Thanks for bringing me home."

Alison smiled and put her arm around Freya's shoulders.

"You know," Max said thoughtfully. "We could always go back, take apart the portal, backtrack to Freya's fortress, and rebuild it there. That might be a faster way to get home. Closer, at least. And who knows who we'll find along the way?"

"No!" the other two shouted in unison.

EPILOGUE,
OR WHEN WE KNOW THE STORY ISN'T OVER

From the Journal of Journals
By Alison

I've transcribed most of Nicholas's journals here, making notes where
I know his recipes to be flawed. (Despite his objections.) I've also made
notes about Grandma Dia's (or "Boots's") journals, but haven't fully
transcribed them because that would just be copying an already clean
journal. I have some room left over for my own thoughts, which is very
lucky.

Our adventures in the Nether were trying and hard, but we found so
much more than we anticipated. I found out more about Grandma Dia.
We met Freya. We saved Uncle Nicholas.

Tomorrow we leave for home. We were an arguing band of two when we
started, now we're a respectable group of five, if you count a certain
somewolf. Nicholas said he thinks it's going to be an easy trip. But so
much of this was supposed to be easy. I've got my doubts.

But while I doubt that our adventure is far from over, I will say that
I'm no longer afraid of what we will encounter. After what we've been
through together, the five of us can handle anything.

MUR LAFFERTY is an award-winning author and Hall of Fame podcaster. She's the author of the Nebula- and Hugo-nominated Best Novel finalist *Six Wakes*, the Shambling Guides series, and *Solo: A Star Wars Story*, and host of the popular *Ditch Diggers* and *I Should Be Writing* podcasts. She also coedits the Hugo-nominated podcast magazine *Escape Pod*.

She lives with her husband, daughter, and two dogs in Durham, North Carolina, where she runs, plays computer and board games, and bakes bread.

murverse.com

ABOUT THE TYPE

This book was set in Electra, a typeface designed for Linotype by renowned type designer W. A. Dwiggins (1880–1956). Electra is a fluid typeface, avoiding the contrasts of thick and thin strokes that are prevalent in most modern typefaces.

JOURNEY INTO THE WORLD OF

MINECRAFT™

—BOOKS FOR EVERY READING LEVEL—

OFFICIAL NOVELS:

MINECRAFT THE ISLAND — MAX BROOKS

MINECRAFT THE MOUNTAIN — MAX BROOKS

MINECRAFT DUNGEONS: THE RISE OF THE ARCH-ILLAGER — MATT FORBECK

MINECRAFT THE SHIPWRECK — C. B. LEE

MINECRAFT THE VOYAGE — JASON FRY

FOR YOUNGER READERS:

OFFICIAL GUIDES:

DISCOVER MORE AT READMINECRAFT.COM

Penguin
Random
House